REVENGE, RECOVERY, AND RESCUE:
THE 3 R MURDERS

Volume 9: Zen and the Art of Investigation

ANTHONY WOLFF

authorHOUSE®

AuthorHouse™
1663 Liberty Drive
Bloomington, IN 47403
www.authorhouse.com
Phone: 1-800-839-8640

This is a work of fiction. All of the characters, names, incidents, organizations, and dialogue
in this novel are either the products of the author's imagination or are used fictitiously.

Published by AuthorHouse 06/17/2014

ISBN: 978-1-4969-1284-8 (sc)
ISBN: 978-1-4969-1283-1 (e)

PREFACE

WHO ARE THESE DETECTIVES ANYWAY?

"The eye cannot see itself" an old Zen adage informs us. The Private I's in these case files count on the truth of that statement. People may be self-concerned, but they are rarely self-aware.

In courts of law, guilt or innocence often depends upon its presentation. Juries do not - indeed, they may not - investigate any evidence in order to test its veracity. No, they are obliged to evaluate only what they are shown. Private Investigators, on the other hand, are obliged to look beneath surfaces and to prove to their satisfaction - not the court's - whether or not what appears to be true is actually true. The Private I must have a penetrating eye.

Intuition is a spiritual gift and this, no doubt, is why *Wagner & Tilson, Private Investigators* does its work so well.

At first glance the little group of P.I.s who solve these often baffling cases seem different from what we (having become familiar with video Dicks) consider "sleuths." They have no oddball sidekicks. They are not alcoholics. They get along well with cops.

George Wagner is the only one who was trained for the job. He obtained a degree in criminology from Temple University in Philadelphia and did exemplary work as a investigator with the Philadelphia Police. These were his golden years. He skied; he danced; he played tennis; he had a Porche, a Labrador retriever, and a small sailboat. He got married and had a wife, two toddlers, and a house. He was handsome and well built, and he had great hair.

And then one night, in 1999, he and his partner walked into an ambush. His partner was killed and George was shot in the left knee and in his right shoulder's brachial plexus. The pain resulting from his injuries and the twenty-two surgeries he endured throughout the year that followed, left him addicted to a nearly constant morphine drip. By the time he was admitted to a rehab center in Southern California for treatment of his morphine addiction and for physical therapy, he had lost everything previously mentioned except his house, his handsome face, and his great hair.

His wife, tired of visiting a semi-conscious man, divorced him and married a man who had more than enough money to make child support payments unnecessary and, since he was the jealous type, undesirable. They moved far away, and despite the calls George placed and the money and gifts he sent, they soon tended to regard him as non-existent. His wife did have an orchid collection which she boarded with a plant nursery, paying for the plants' care until he was able to accept them. He gave his brother his car, his tennis racquets, his skis, and his sailboat.

At the age of thirty-four he was officially disabled, his right arm and hand had begun to wither slightly from limited use, a frequent result of a severe injury to that nerve center. His knee, too, was troublesome. He could not hold it in a bent position for an extended period of time; and when the weather was bad or he had been standing for too long, he limped a little.

George gave considerable thought to the "disease" of romantic love and decided that he had acquired an immunity to it. He would never again be vulnerable to its delirium. He did not realize that the gods of love regard such pronouncements as hubris of the worst kind and, as such, never allow it to go unpunished. George learned this lesson while working on the case, *The Monja Blanca*. A sweet girl, half his age and nearly half his weight, would fell him, as he put it, "as young David slew the big dumb Goliath." He understood that while he had no future with her, his future would be filled with her for as long as he had a mind that could think. She had been the victim of the most vicious swindlers he had ever encountered. They had successfully fled the country, but not the range of George's determination to apprehend them. These were master criminals, four of them, and he secretly vowed that he would make them fall, one by one. This was a serious quest. There was nothing quixotic about George Roberts Wagner.

While he was in the hospital receiving treatment for those fateful gunshot wounds, he met Beryl Tilson.

Beryl, a widow whose son Jack was then eleven years old, was working her way through college as a nurse's aid when she tended George. She had met him previously when he delivered a lecture on the curious differences between aggravated assault and attempted murder, a not uninteresting topic. During the year she tended him, they became friendly enough for him to communicate with her during the year he was in rehab. When he returned to Philadelphia, she picked him up at the airport, drove him home - to a house he had not been inside for two years - and helped him to get settled into a routine with the house and the botanical spoils of his divorce.

After receiving her degree in the Liberal Arts, Beryl tried to find a job with hours that would permit her to be home when her son came home from school each day. Her quest was daunting. Not only was a degree in Liberal Arts regarded as a 'negative' when considering an applicant's qualifications, (the choice of study having demonstrated a lack of foresight for eventual entry into the commercial job market) but by stipulating that she needed to be home no later than 3:30 p.m. each day, she further discouraged personnel managers from putting out their company's welcome mat. The supply of available jobs was somewhat limited.

Beryl, a Zen Buddhist and karate practitioner, was still doing part-time work when George proposed that they open a private investigation agency. Originally he had thought she would function as a "girl friday" office manager; but when he witnessed her abilities in the martial arts, which, at that time, far exceeded his, he agreed that she should function as a 50-50 partner in the agency, and he helped her through the licensing procedure. She quickly became an excellent marksman on the gun range.

As a Christmas gift he gave her a Beretta to use alternately with her Colt semi-automatic.

The Zen temple she attended was located on Germantown Avenue in a two storey, store-front row of small businesses. Wagner & Tilson, Private Investigators needed a home. Beryl noticed that a building in the same row was advertised for sale. She told George who liked it, bought it, and let Beryl and her son move into the second floor as their residence. Problem solved.

While George considered himself a man's man, Beryl did not see herself as a woman's woman. She had no female friends her own age. None. Acquaintances, yes. She enjoyed warm relationships with a few older women. But Beryl, it surprised her to realize, was a man's woman. She liked men, their freedom to move, to create, to discover, and that inexplicable wildness that came with their physical presence and strength. All of her senses found them agreeable; but she had no desire to domesticate one. Going to sleep with one was nice. But waking up with one of them in her bed? No. No. No. Dawn had an alchemical effect on her sensibilities. "Colors seen by candlelight do not look the same by day," said Elizabeth Barrett Browning, to which Beryl replied, "Amen."

She would find no occasion to alter her orisons until, in the course of solving a missing person's case that involved sexual slavery in a South American rainforest, a case called *Skyspirit,* she met the Surinamese Southern District's chief criminal investigator. Dawn became conducive to romance. But, as we all know, the odds are always against the success of long distance love affairs. To be stuck in one continent and love a man who is stuck in another holds as much promise for high romance as falling in love with Dorian Gray. In her professional life, she was tough but fair. In matters of lethality, she preferred *dim mak* points to bullets, the latter being awfully messy.

Perhaps the most unusual of the three detectives is Sensei Percy Wong. The reader may find it useful to know a bit more about his background.

Sensei, Beryl's karate master, left his dojo to go to Taiwan to become a fully ordained Zen Buddhist priest in the Ummon or Yun Men lineage in which he was given the Dharma name Shi Yao Feng. After studying advanced martial arts in both Taiwan and China, he returned to the U.S. to teach karate again and to open a small Zen Buddhist temple - the temple that was down the street from the office *Wagner & Tilson* would eventually open.

Sensei was quickly considered a great martial arts' master not because, as he explains, "I am good at karate, but because I am better at advertising it." He was of Chinese descent and had been ordained in China, and since China's Chan Buddhism and Gung Fu stand in polite rivalry to Japan's Zen Buddhism and Karate, it was most peculiar to find a priest in China's Yun Men lineage who followed the Japanese Zen liturgy and the martial arts discipline of Karate.

It was only natural that Sensei Percy Wong's Japanese associates proclaimed that his preferences were based on merit, and in fairness to them, he did not care to disabuse them of this notion. In truth, it was Sensei's childhood rebellion against his tyrannical faux-Confucian father that caused him to gravitate to the Japanese forms. Though both of his parents had emigrated from China, his father decried western civilization even as he grew rich exploiting its freedoms and commercial opportunities. With draconian finesse he imposed upon his family the cultural values of the country from which he had fled for his life. He seriously believed that while the rest of the world's population might have come out of Africa, Chinese men came out of heaven. He did not know or care where Chinese women originated so long as they kept their proper place as slaves.

His mother, however, marveled at American diversity and refused to speak Chinese to her children, believing, as she did, in the old fashioned idea that it is wise to speak the language of the country in which one claims citizenship.

At every turn the dear lady outsmarted her obsessively sinophilic husband. Forced to serve rice at every meal along with other mysterious creatures obtained in Cantonese Chinatown, she purchased two Shar Peis that, being from Macau, were given free rein of the dining room. These dogs, despite their pre-Qin dynasty lineage, lacked a discerning palate and proved to be gluttons for bowls of fluffy white stuff. When her husband retreated to his rooms, she served omelettes and Cheerios, milk instead of tea, and at dinner, when he was not there at all, spaghetti instead of chow mein. The family home was crammed with gaudy enameled furniture and torturously carved teak; but on top of the lion-head-ball-claw-legged coffee table, she always placed a book which illustrated the elegant simplicity of such furniture designers as Marcel Breuer; Eileen Gray; Charles Eames; and American Shakers. Sensei adored her; and loved to hear her relate how, when his father ordered her to give their firstborn son a Chinese name; she secretly asked the clerk to record indelibly the name "Percy" which she mistakenly thought was a very American name. To Sensei, if she had named him Abraham Lincoln Wong, she could not have given him a more Yankee handle.

Preferring the cuisines of Italy and Mexico, Sensei avoided Chinese food and prided himself on not knowing a word of Chinese. He balanced this ignorance by an inability to understand Japanese and, because of its inaccessibility, he did not eat Japanese food.

The Man of Zen who practices Karate obviously is the adventurous type; and Sensei, staying true to type, enjoyed participating in Beryl's and George's investigations. It required little time for him to become a one-third partner of the team. He called himself, "the ampersand in *Wagner & Tilson.*"

Sensei Wong may have been better at advertising karate than at performing it, but this merely says that he was a superb huckster for the discipline. In college he had studied civil engineering; but he also was on the fencing team and he regularly practiced gymnastics. He had learned yoga and ancient forms of meditation from his mother. He attained Zen's vaunted transcendental states; which he could access 'on the mat.' It was not surprising that when he began to learn karate he was already half-accomplished. After he won a few minor championships he attracted the attention of several martial arts publications that found his "unprecedented" switchings newsworthy. They imparted to him a "great master" cachet, and perpetuated it to the delight of dojo owners and martial arts shopkeepers. He did win many championships and, through unpaid endorsements and political propaganda, inspired the sale of Japanese weapons, including nunchaku and shuriken which he did not actually use.

Although his Order was strongly given to celibacy, enough wiggle room remained for the priest who found it expedient to marry or dally. Yet, having reached his mid-forties unattached, he regarded it as 'unlikely' that he would ever be romantically welded to a female, and as 'impossible' that he would be bonded to a citizen and custom's agent of the People's Republic of China - whose Gung Fu abilities challenged him and who would strike terror in his heart especially when she wore Manolo Blahnik red spike heels. Such combat, he insisted, was patently unfair, but he prayed that Providence would not level the playing field. He met his femme fatale while working on *A Case of Virga*.

Later in their association Sensei would take under his spiritual wing a young Thai monk who had a degree in computer science and a flair for acting. Akara Chatree, to whom Sensei's master in Taiwan would give the name Shi Yao Xin, loved Shakespeare; but his father - who came from one of Thailand's many noble families - regarded his son's desire to become an actor as we would regard our son's desire to become a hit man. Akara's brothers were all businessmen and professionals; and as the old patriarch lay dying, he exacted a promise from his tall 'matinee-idol' son that he would never tread upon the flooring of a stage. The old man had asked for nothing else, and since he bequeathed a rather large sum of money to his young son, Akara had to content himself with critiquing the performances of actors who were less filially constrained than he. As far as romance is concerned, he had not thought too much about it until he worked on *A Case of Industrial Espionage*. That case took him to Bermuda, and what can a young hero do when he is captivated by a pretty girl who can recite Portia's lines with crystalline insight while lying beside him on a white beach near a blue ocean?

But his story will keep...

BEFORE THE ACTION BEGINS...

It is a definition of Karma that every action causes an infinity of effects which, in turn, create an infinity of causes. This is the material world's great network of interconnecting lines and knots from which no single line or knot can be removed without creating a chaotic breach in the flow of time and light.

Yet, despite the impossibility of tracing back a single effect to a single cause, human nature allows for no other response to an event. Intellectually, an array of causes for any event may be acknowledged; but emotionally, where the movement occurs, there is always a determined effort to isolate an effect's cause and to appropriate praise or blame to it.

Science marches on, but human nature is eternally a spectator standing on the sidewalk, watching the parade. The notion that as a species we are evolving into wise creatures in tandem with our scientific advancements is a material-world fiction. The mechanisms of ego-consciousness imprison us in the emotional point-counterpoint of praise and blame, of desire and aversion, and of happiness and misery.

It is only when the ego and its veil of illusion are obliterated that in a dazzling moment the mind can expand into the real world's Unity and apprehend fully the lasting joy, truth, peace, and freedom that exist only there.

This transcendent moment rarely occurs. In Zen it is called Satori.

Although Spiritual Healer Juan deJesus Tolavera would never have admitted that his patient's wealth influenced him to conduct her treatment outside the confines of an acceptable therapeutic regimen (even for a shaman) it had become increasingly apparent that his much

1

heralded cures of Margaret Cioran were invariably followed by quiet relapses, and that this dismal record of failure had prompted the highly regarded *curandero* to resort to unorthodox and somewhat expensive methods to relieve her "spiritual" distress.

In the fall of 2009, Margaret had been the victim of a cruel "marriage/blackmail" swindle. Lilyanne Smith had been similarly victimized a few months later - and by the same four "suspected" swindlers; but while Lily seemed to have recovered from the ordeal, Margaret was plunged into an obdurate depression.

Lilyanne credited her recovery to prayer, reflection, adherence to the Christian mandate to forgive, and to a long Pacific cruise. She hoped that Margaret would follow her example, but Margaret's case was more serious and could not be managed by philosophy and sea voyages. She had become addicted to anti-depression medications.

After a medical intervention which saw her through a difficult withdrawal, Margaret remained in a lifeless state of malaise. A neighbor recommended that Juan deJesus Tolavera be consulted. The *curandero* spent an hour with the unfortunate girl and pronounced her, "A sealed vessel that contained no joy"; and he assured her parents that he would not fail to break that seal and to open Margaret's vessel to the bliss of cosmic consciousness. His price for the initial two-month effort was a hundred thousand dollars which, he noted, included air fare to his retreat in Mazatlan. Considering the assured outcome, it seemed to be a bargain; and Margaret entered the retreat.

In May of 2010 she began a series of cures and relapses. She would come home for a month or two of halcyon days in which she would seem to have regained her sweet disposition and composure, but then she would lapse into depression and would have to return to the Tolavera Retreat. Lilyanne, visiting regularly with Margaret, objected to the "new age" techniques the *curandero* employed to effect these respites. She pleaded with Margaret's father to transfer her to a reputable medical facility, but Cioran had refused, believing that all that was required to effect a permanent cure was to lengthen these "normal" stretches, and that regardless of the methods the *curandero* employed, he was getting results.

Under Tolavera's direction, Margaret purchased an electrically illuminated crystal statue of a god that had the head and antlers of a deer - a well-known archaic divinity. The technique required that each evening, in her darkened room, she sip a cup of Tolavera's special tea, stare into the light beams imprisoned in the statue, and follow their path into a delirious trance state. While in this supra-normal locus, she was to pray to the icon, beseeching it to use its antlers to annihilate the handsome Henri La Fontaine who had betrayed her. Her mind's eye would see her champion pierce and rend La Fontaine's body; and then, when its rage abated, she would watch its antlers relax into dreadlocks and its cervidae features morph into those of a handsome man possessed of a rather sexy human body who sauntered into her bedroom.

After she had watched the god dispatch La Fontaine a few dozen times, her rage would also abate and she would return home with a small supply of special tea bags and, without disclosing the true purpose of the statue, she would plug it in and continue her nocturnal adventures. Her daily interactions were those of her old sweet self and her parents were too relieved to question such a blessing.

But then Margaret would discover that no matter how she increased the wattage or how she varied the beseeching prayer, nothing would happen. With or without tea, she had "habituated" to the technique - a frequent impasse encountered by those who meditate with or without hypnotic aids - and the euphoria she once felt slid into chthonian depths from which no stag or human ravisher could emerge. Once again, she would be plunged into depression and would be transported to Tolavera's retreat. A new meditative object - lion-headed Aion accompanied by recorded flute music, Hathor observed while shaking a sistrum, and so on - and new meditative techniques of rhythm, light, and shape would be given her along with stronger tea, and the process would begin again.

It frequently happens that people who have not actually experienced an illness attribute their cure of it to certain measures they have taken. Lilyanne Smith, who had spent five years in a Catholic convent before her disastrous engagement, so believed that the peace she had attained was attributable to her Christian principles that when Private Investigator George Wagner vowed, in a personal commitment to her, to bring her four antagonists to justice, she absolutely forbade any act of retribution, admonishing Wagner that if *she* could forgive them, he certainly ought to be able to do so. Forgiveness was then the essential tool by which true peace could be fashioned from conflict. Lilyanne Smith knew next to nothing about Post Traumatic Stress Disorder.

In the spring of 2011 Stephen Cioran tearfully called to tell her that Margaret had attempted suicide and was currently in intensive care in a Seattle hospital. "I have been too ashamed of myself for not listening to you," he said, "but for the love of heaven, please help us. My wife and I are beyond rational thought."

Lilyanne took the next flight to Seattle. She sat beside the comatose girl for three days, and on the fourth day Margaret opened her eyes. Somewhere in the depths of her ordeal, a divine thumb was turned and the ego's veil was finally lifted. She saw the world unitively for the first time.

She confided to Lily, "Before I look ahead, I want to understand the history of my failure. Can you help me to do this?" Lilyanne responded by calling the abbess of the convent in which she had once lived to ask if she could recommend a qualified, non-religious source of information that would assist her friend. She told the abbess about Margaret's adventures with the spiritual healer and the hypnotically induced delusions that ended in attempted suicide. The abbess gave her the name of a teacher of Jungian thought who lived in Seattle. Margaret went to him regularly for lessons and discussions which greatly helped her integration into normal social life. As a safety measure, she also met once a week with a board-certified psychiatrist. Lilyanne, meanwhile, went on another extended "health and yoga" cruise of the South Pacific with her mother who had become an avid yoga enthusiast following Lily's romantic catastrophe.

In 2011, Margaret enjoyed Thanksgiving Dinner with her family. She also spent the Christmas and New Year holidays skiing with Lilyanne and two male friends of her own genus and species at her family's ski lodge in Idaho. Before the clock struck midnight, she called Lily aside. "I can't start the New Year without telling you how sorry I am that I didn't stop Henri La Fontaine when I had the chance. Fear and pride imprisoned me and left him free to victimize you. I'm responsible for your misery and yet you came and helped me." She looked at Lilyanne Smith and two tears spilled from her eyes. Lilyanne, profoundly moved, handed her a tissue. "It is over," she said, "and we can put it in the past." She did not realize that while "it" might have ended for Margaret, "it" had yet to begin for her.

In January 2012, Lilyanne had a violent nightmare about Henri La Fontaine and his three fellow conspirators. She dreamed that she was in a burning building and they were chasing her. No matter which corridor she chose to effect her escape, flames blocked the exit. She awakened in a state of terror. Her heart was racing and she could not go back to sleep. The nightmares and panic attacks continued, and she also experienced debilitating headaches that she supposed only salt-air could cure. She called the only residences she knew that her "four tormentors" used, but they were not at home in any of them. Impulsively she booked passage on a Caribbean cruise, on a ship that happened to stop at Grand Cayman Island.

Lilyanne Smith knew that the Cayman Islands was a country that she ought to avoid. In the scheme that had victimized her, large donations that were obviously blackmail payments had to be made "as penance" to a charity that used the name "Christian Eleemosynary Actions, Ltd." The headquarters of the CEA, Ltd. was in George Town, the capital of the British territory. By stopping, even for only a few hours in the Caymans, she intended to prove to herself that she had long ago prevailed over her tormenters, that some other source of anguish had merely adopted their names and forms, and that her scheduled visit would reaffirm the validity of her Christian efforts. Accordingly, she contacted a private detective in the Caymans and asked what information he could obtain about Henri La Fontaine, his mother Charlotte La Fontaine, Eric Haffner, and a tall, heavily built Jamaican named Martin Shannon.

The detective reported that there was no record of such individuals living in the Islands. She asked him to check-out the executives of CEA, Ltd. He reported that the organization was no longer in existence and that all of the names previously listed were of persons living in Africa except for the two former resident agents, a gentlemen named Martin Williams and his wife Harriet who were well known in the islands. She asked him for photographs and his opinion about the kind of people they were. He assured her that they were quiet, respectable, long-term residents of George Town. "Mrs. Williams does her own housework and rides around town on a bicycle." He sent several photographs of a dowdy, toothy hausfrau who hid behind steel-rimmed glasses as she peddled a three-wheeler bicycle with a basket filled with groceries. "Mr. Williams keeps a sailing ship in the Barcadere Marina. But he got sick and keeps to himself now. I was able to get shots of him because he was going into the out-patient clinic of the Princess Diana Hospital." Mr. Williams was a thin, balding, African American man who walked with a cane and was easily forty years older than the man who appeared in the blackmail photos.

"Do the Williams' have any children... any sons?" she asked.

"No, but sometimes young people from their religious group stay with them to give them a hand."

Lilyanne was satisfied that if Charlotte and Henri had any connection to the CEA, Ltd. it was probably farther down the line, possibly in one of the African countries in which the charity had missions. For all she knew, the two people she saw in the photographs were victims, too.

In mid-January, Lilyanne joined other shipmates who wanted to spend an afternoon in George Town and boarded a tender that took passengers to shore. She was finally able to visit the Barcadere. As she strolled along the wharf she saw a sloop named *Remittman* docked there. She recalled that Henri La Fontaine had referred to a European friend as "a remittance man" and explained the term's meaning as "a troublesome person whose family pays him to stay away from their home territory." A blonde man of approximately 35 years of age appeared on deck, and after glancing in her direction, went down into the cabin. Lilyanne was certain that she had seen Eric Haffner, one of the four swindlers. She trembled with fear, turned away, and began to jog back to the tender. The cruise ship's horn sounded a first warning and she boarded the tender and sat down. She was the first passenger to return.

On the main ship she consulted with the ship's doctor who, seeing the unmistakable signs of a nearly irrational fear, gave her tranquilizers. Her nightmares worsened, and possibly to relieve their pressure on her psyche, during waking hours she would lapse into daydreams about killing Eric. The pills helped to quell this uncomfortable passion.

At the conclusion of the cruise, she had lost weight, looked haggard, and felt worse than when she had started. She checked herself into a Catholic sanitarium in Maryland.

Placed in the care of a Catholic priest who was also a psychiatrist, she was asked to reveal the sordid details of her romantic ordeal; but she insisted that she could not remember them. On the night of her "social catastrophe" she had been drugged and all that she knew of the event she had learned afterwards from hospital reports and from glancing at a few blackmailing photographs of herself and two men, but these images were conflated with those of Margaret Cioran whom she unfortunately referred to as "her sister victim" when speaking to the doctor.

Although drugs had, in fact, prevented her from remembering anything, her physician formed the theory that her inability to recall details was symptomatic of repressed guilt for her having rejected her religious vocation, and that the disaster she described had been self-induced as a form of punishment for abandoning the spiritual life. He insisted that her failures as a Bride of Christ and as a Bride of Henri La Fontaine had the same pathologic origin. Lilyanne Smith regarded this as a personal insult and told the man she would have been better served by a *curandero*, which was a worse criticism than he imagined. She left the facility after only four days of treatment.

She returned to Philadelphia and tried to spend as much time out of the house as possible. She could never predict when she would have an attack of anxiety in which she would stutter and tremble and feel her heart racing.

At the end of January she walked through Fairmount Park and came upon an elderly man who was sitting on a park bench feeding pigeons. Asked if he would mind if she sat down, he smiled and replied that he welcomed the company. They discussed the ethics of feeding pigeons (a not-uncommon topic of controversy among city dwellers) and then discussed ethics in general. "Something is bothering you," he said, "something that you need to talk about. Maybe you should talk to a priest."

Her response was grim. "I tried that and it didn't work." But as she left the park she thought that she didn't necessarily have to talk to a priest of her own religion. There was always Sensei Percy Wong. He was a Zen Buddhist priest. Originally, his personal and professional closeness to George Wagner had inhibited her from contacting him; but now she thought that perhaps his knowledge of the details of her ordeal might be beneficial providing, of course, that their communications were kept private.

She called Sensei at the little Zen temple located down the street from the office of Wagner & Tilson, Private Investigators. When he answered, she asked, "Sensei, are you alone?"

He recognized her voice. "Lilyanne! Yes, I'm here in the temple kitchen and I'm alone."

"I need to talk to you but I don't want anyone else to enter our conversation."

"I understand. Well, I can tell you that if you come here, there's no telling when we'll get company. How about if I drive to wherever you are and we get some coffee or tea and discuss privately whatever you want to talk about."

"Are you obliged to keep whatever I tell you confidential?"

"I'm obliged. But if I think your life is in danger and only I can provide the information that will save your life - and I'm absolutely convinced of that - then I can't ethically stand by and watch you perish when I know I could have helped to save you. Is that what you want to know?"

"Yes. All right, then... let's hope it never comes to that. Can you meet me in the park?" She gave him directions.

Sensei took one look at her and exclaimed, "You may need a physician more than you need a priest! Let's go and get you some solid food. Italian?"

As they walked to his car, he asked, "How long have you had 'the shakes'?"

She began to outline everything that had happened to her and to Margaret during the last two years.

Throughout her lengthy narrative, she managed to eat. She was eating absentmindedly, chatting with someone, paying no attention to what she was doing.

Over dessert, he discussed the difficulties of the problem. "We'll need more than a few conversations to get you through this. The course is a rough one. You're having a delayed response to a disastrous event. Think of it as the incubation period of a disease. Time doesn't mean anything because each disease is different. As each human being is different each incidence of betrayal is also unique. There is no 'one size fits all' remedy.

"The first thing that a person has to do is to stop seeing the betrayer as 100% guilty and the betrayed as 100% innocent. The first difficult step is to look objectively at the event. Unless a person can see his or her own participation - however small that participation was - there can't be any progress. There's a big difference in being an abused infant and an abused adult. The infant has no ego that is trying to manipulate events in any degree. Without an ego's involvement, there is purity, and a pure victim doesn't crave satisfaction. The disorder we're speaking about is one of an abused ego. A person who was injured or insulted was not given the opportunity to strike back at the person who harmed him, to even the score. He sees himself as being laughed at or neglected, or as being an object of pity or scorn. He wants to be seen as bold, brave, and intelligent and circumstance won't permit that.

"The place to start is to take your mind back to the event. Ask yourself if you or your parents contributed in any way to the disaster. Did you choose to overlook clues that something was wrong? Were you ever wary - as we are told we should be - when something appeared to be 'too good to be true'? Despite any misgivings, were you and your parents so eager to attain your own objective - in this case, marriage to a handsome nobleman who said he loved you - that you silenced the small voice in your head that doubted that everything was in fact as it was presented to you?"

Lilyanne sighed. "I've thought about this and I even remember my own change in attitude. In the convent, we strove to be as plain as possible, as simple and unadorned as a soul should be before God. And suddenly I was actively engaged in trying to get someone to do what I wanted in the same way that a fisherman baits a hook. I bought dresses that I intended he should admire. I had my hair done to look more attractive. I wore perfume to be more alluring. And my parents 'bent over backwards' trying to accommodate the expectations. So, in a real sense, we encouraged the abuse. And yes, there were plenty of signs that something was wrong and we all just didn't want to read the signs."

Sensei smiled. "If you can keep this objectivity, you'll prevail. You're thinking constructively now. The first step is to accept responsibility for your contribution - however small - to the problem you now have. So, you were abused. Smarter people than you have been duped by dumber people than those four swindlers. And those victims lost more. Some are even dead. You're still here. You're a survivor.

"The next step is more difficult. It doesn't deal with your little part in the problem. It deals exclusively with your response to the main culprit, the person or persons who betrayed you, stole from you, humiliated you, and committed a terrible crime against you.

"You have a victim's ethical and social dilemma. You want justice, but the price of getting it is telling the world how you allowed yourself to be duped. And that isn't easy to do especially if you feel that you've already suffered enough. And what's worse, you've been abused and you're religiously expected to forgive the people who hurt you and you're socially required to do nothing outside the law. Unfortunately, they have not asked you for forgiveness. So when you forgive, you are, in effect, requiring yourself to pretend that what they did is excusable, is pardonable. This might ennoble you, but it will have no effect on them, except, of course, to remove the annoyance of having to deal with someone who seeks justice or revenge. What they did was a crime. You can't or you won't go to the police and charge them with blackmail, since the evidence of blackmail is the blackmail, itself. And if you did know where they were located and went there to complain, the authorities would not believe you once they were shown the pictures - which must have been convincing since your father did, after all, pay the money. Your complaints would be turned against you. Blackmailers count on this.

"So, Lilyanne, someone you loved betrayed you for money. It's an old story. For two years you prided yourself on having gotten past this dark episode. Your soul cried out for justice, and your brain told it to be quiet and thought it would obey. It wouldn't. You're suffering from Post Traumatic Stress Disorder. Somebody hurt you or scared you, but civilization prevents you from obtaining satisfaction for those injuries, and your ego wants that balance restored. You are now at war with yourself."

He advised her to go home and consider what he had said and to call him as soon as she reached a conclusion about his description of her situation.

She pondered her new lower rank among victims, her efforts to attract her abuser, and her blindness to clues of perfidy that were clearly obvious. That night her dreams were a jumbled mess of being found naked in situations in which clothing was preferred.

The next week she was ready to discuss what Sensei considered the most important question of all. He asked, "Given that you cannot legally stop the four swindlers, and assuming that they will victimize other innocent persons, what is your responsibility regarding their career of crime? This is the question that stumps everybody. The decision requires conviction of such magnitude that any and all possible consequences must be accepted before you do or say anything about the problem. You must be certain of their intransigent guilt."

Lilyanne thought of Margaret Cioran's apology for not taking action against her abusers. She listened to Sensei, but everything he said she began to re-interpret in terms of Margaret's experience.

"Let's consider cases," Sensei said. "You are on a passenger ship that capsizes, and you, five little children, and a man get washed up on a deserted island. The man catches fish. You gather coconuts. You see certain marks of abuse on the children and you learn that he is sexually molesting them. What is your responsibility? Go home and call me when you have an answer."

Lilyanne Smith's thoughts struggled with passion and reason. Her dreams continued to be fearful and the element of nakedness remained. In another week, she called and said that she was ready to discuss the problem. She had not reached an answer at all; but, eager to resolve her problem, she thought about it and assumed that she had given it the consideration it deserved. Meeting with Sensei she said, "The kind of man who will molest children is not the kind of man who will listen to my pleas to cease abusing them. If I protest, he could destroy me and do as he wishes with the children."

"Now either you do nothing and remain safe while the children continue to be abused, or you act to protect them. What do you do?"

"I know I'm supposed to say that I should devise a way to kill or incapacitate him so that he will not continue to molest the children."

"No," Sensei countered. "You're not supposed to suppose anything. You're supposed to think independently and not rely on the expectations of religion or society."

"My years of spiritual discipline forbid harmful actions. We never really thought about real-life situations when we extolled the 'do no harm' route. Does 'do no harm' ultimately mean that we prevent ourselves from being harmed by ignoring the problem? It's even possible that we could change and cultivate a *laissez faire* attitude towards the children's suffering. Worse, we might inhibit others from punishing those who will continue to harm them. After all, religious people have been known to fall into the arms of sin when they come face to face with it.

"It might be that natural forces or civil forces will stop him, obviating the need to act. He could drown while fishing, or die, or become disabled because of natural circumstances, or he might have an epiphany of sorts and yield to a divine command to cease doing wrong. Even the most hardened criminal may experience a conversion. It might also be that a rescue party comes to the island and he is automatically stopped.

"The 'forgive and do no harm' approach comes very close to cowardice masquerading as morality. It does not reach the level of cowardice because there is still that margin of change - be it natural, divine, or otherwise."

Sensei listened to her and was disheartened to hear how she was removing herself from the specific problem and its solution. "*You* must stay focussed on *your* problem. *You* are on the island with the helpless victims and the victimizer. *You* are the one who must consider possibilities. Either the man will continue exactly as he has been doing, or he will change for the better, or he will change for the worse. You must observe him objectively and decide which course is the most likely, and also what the consequences of each course will be for you and for the children. You must act on thoroughly considered possibilities. So, what do *you* do?"

Lilyanne shook her head and again let herself ascend to Margaret's enlightened position. "I know that if I believe that he is continuing or getting worse, he must be stopped; and if I choose not to interfere, then the next time he commits this same crime, I am complicit in the act."

She began to add her own details to someone else's "discovery." "I recall a case," she said, "that involved this very problem. Where I live, a male hospital nurse was fired for unnamed acts he had committed; but when he applied for a position with another hospital, the man who fired him gave him an acceptable reference because he didn't want to risk a law suit. The nurse went on to commit even more serious crimes and was arrested. The man who gave him an acceptable reference lost his job. Most people thought he should have been punished more severely. But what would have happened to him if he had been honest? The law requires proof. And God help the person who makes a charge and cannot prove it to the satisfaction of the legal authorities. He is the one who will be sacrificed."

"You've outlined the dilemma. As you regard the consequences, immobility would seem to be the moralist's *tarantella*. But you still haven't told me what *you'd* do when you were alone on the island with the victims and the victimizer, and the only law enforcement was directed by your conscience."

Unable to slip out of the spotlight, Lilyanne had to acknowledge that she had not reached any conclusions at all. "I'm stumbling around in the dark. I need more time to think about this."

"Restate the problem in the terms applicable to religious principles, not to a civil code. If you forgive the criminal and he commits the same crime again, you are complicit in the crime. Or, if unknown to you, he has repented of his crimes and has been forgiven by God, and since that moment of salvation he has not erred again, and you act to destroy him, then you have sinned when you harmed him. You must be convinced of his status. Call me when you reach a conclusion." He gave her a book that contained the lectures of a Chinese Zen Buddhist saint. "If you need help, this might give you some pointers."

Lilyanne Smith put the book in her tote bag. As she got up to leave she turned to Sensei. "Theoretical Ethics is a joke. I now have to re-think my entire philosophy. I'll call again when I decide what is the right thing for me to do."

"*Omitofo!*" said Sensei. "I look forward to seeing you get started on Enlightenment's Path."

Lilyanne Smith, however, did not want to start at the beginning of the Path. She wanted to start at the end. And in this, she was no different from nearly all others who Quest.

FRIDAY, FEBRUARY 17, 2012

The sun was bright. The sky was blue. The breeze was cool and gentle. There was much to see and hear on the streets of George Town: music from brightly colored kiosks, shouts of pushcart vendors, souvenir hucksters, and the pointed arguments of barristers who wore black robes and curly white horsehair wigs as they clustered near the court.

Lilyanne Smith squinted against the sunlight as she left the Lamark Hotel's lobby. She put on her sunglasses and bent her sun hat's wire-lined brim down to shade her face. She enjoyed the pleasant streets as she seemed to be nonchalantly padding along in the direction of the quay; but she was in deadly earnest as she reached the pier beside which she had once seen the Remittman docked. The berth was empty now. She looked over the side into the clear water, noticing the mussels and barnacles that clung to the pilings. Finding them not lively enough to sustain interest, she swung her tote bag around, looking for something to look at.

She wore a halter top, a full length flouncy skirt, and huarache sandals. In appearance, she blended in with the hundreds of tourists from dozens of nations who strolled along the capital's clean and bustling streets. Her objectives, however, were different from all others. She was on a mission of confrontation that she hoped would occur at the Barcadere Marina. She had no weapon or plan and no expectation that she would even see anyone she knew. But if nothing happened on that day, she would wait for another... and another. She was not on a cruise ship's schedule and she was not oppressed by time.

Towards the end of the pier she saw a sailboat, its sails furled, using its small engine to come alongside slowly. She could not identify the type of sailboat it was - it had a single mast and at least a crew of three.

15

One of the crewmen jumped onto the dock as another threw him a line. Bumpers had been hung over the side of the vessel, and the captain, listening to the man on the pier who called out measurements in Spanish, eased the boat against the dock as the crewman tied the line to a cleat.

Lilyanne walked to the stern to read its name. It was Santiago, out of Havana. She took particular interest in the crewman who had tossed the line. He wore a gun belt. The captain and the man who was already on the pier left the vessel and nodded to her as they passed. Lilyanne watched them leave and then turned and smiled broadly at the crewman who stayed aboard to guard the ship.

"Señorita," he said, acknowledging her presence, and then he went below, and she turned and walked back to the wharf, reading off the names of the ships she passed and wondering if any of them belonged to the "vicious four."

"How," she asked herself, "am I going to do this thing?" It surprised her that she had not considered "the means" of her mission, if, indeed, she had a mission at all. "If it is Haffner, then he is either reformed or as evil as before. He might pretend that he's reformed, but I think I've had enough experience to tell the difference between spiritual sincerity and a fake show of piety. But if he is his same old evil self? If I'm ever to regain my own peace of mind, I'll have to put him out of his misery. But how? Poison his drink? Push him overboard in the middle of a shark filled ocean? Shoot him? The gun belt on the ship's crewman continued to interest her. "I will have to let the story unfold," she whispered to herself. "Que será será." She approached a vendor who sold pineapple juice drinks, bought two, and walked back to the Santiago.

"Ahoy! Santiago!" she called. The crewman's head appeared and then, seeing the two plastic cups in her hands, he smiled and continued to climb up from the cabin. He grabbed the rail and stretched towards her so that she could hand him the cups. One at a time, he put them on the hatch, and then he put the boarding ladder over the side. She began to climb it, and as she reached the top, he grabbed her and in one swift movement he had his arm around her waist and lifted her over the rail and onto the deck. She laughed as he sat her beside the pineapple drinks.

Then he took one drink and said, "*Gracias*. This is just what I need. What's your name?"

She answered truthfully. She had her passport in her tote bag and knew that if he decided to check her identity for himself, he could easily do it. But when he asked, "What brings you to the Caymans?" she gave an answer that was not entirely true. "Oh, a few years ago a couple of people who are from around here borrowed a large amount of money from my father and they never paid it back. I always felt responsible for that. I'm the one who brought them home. So, I guess I just wanted to see if they had done anything honorable with the money."

"And you looked for them here? On this pier?"

"Yes, I think one has a sailboat called Remittman."

"I know the ship! White hull. Blonde guy. My age: *treinta y seis*. What's his name?"

"I don't know the name he uses down here. He moves around, hard to catch. A slippery guy."

He laughed. "I've seen him and I know what you mean. In Cuba we say, 'Él es tan resbaladizo como una semilla de sandía.' You understand?"

"Yes... he's slippery like a watermelon seed."

"You love this guy?"

"God, no!"

"His brother?"

"You mean another blonde guy... same size, same age?"

"Yeah, that's the one."

"No. He's a devil."

"I didn't think you would be in love with that one. He likes boys. You know what I mean?"

Lilyanne Smith did not have any idea that Henri La Fontaine "likes boys." She was suddenly awestruck by the magnitude of his deceit. All that business about getting engaged and living "ever after" in some happy home with their children. Her hands were suddenly cold and she realized that she had been holding her breath. She forced herself to take a deep breath. "Ah," she finally said, "I wasn't in love with either of them." She gulped down half of her pineapple drink. "So tell me, how is it that you get to know other ship owners?"

"I don't own this ship. I work for my boss. He comes here twice a month on private business. I don't have a passport so I can't leave the ship. But that doesn't matter. My job is to guard the ship while he and the first mate are ashore."

"How long do you stay each time?"

"Usually, we leave Trinidad, Cuba on the first and arrive here on the third. Then we go back on the 5th. So we're here two nights. Because of the wind, it usually takes twice as long to get here as it does to get back. The Jefe conducts his business and spends the nights with friends. But the mate, he's got a girlfriend he sees. Got a couple of kids by her. Then we leave Cuba again on the fifteenth, get here on the eighteenth, and go back on the twentieth."

"And since you stay on the ship, you know what goes on with the local sailing crowd."

"I got no television. What else can I do? And that Remittman ship, it's a little entertaining. Strange people. I'd see them almost every time we were here. And then I wouldn't see them again for months. I haven't seen the ship this trip, but last trip the owner was busy loading stuff on the ship."

"What kind of stuff?"

"Furniture and building supplies. I don't talk to him, so I don't know what they are. But that's what it looks like. I've seen paint cans and a ladder and roofing tiles."

"I wish I knew what name he was using. It sounds like he's renovating a house... somewhere close."

"I can tell you that he sails east-northeast so that says to me, Little Cayman or Cayman Brac. We know he isn't heading for Cuba!" He laughed.

Lilyanne smiled at his little joke. "You didn't tell me your name," she complained.

"It's Leonardo. Leonardo Arenas."

"Why don't you have a passport, Leonardo?"

"You ask a lot of questions, Señorita. But I've spent half my life considering myself an American so you can ask me whatever you want. Staying here in solitary confinement would make a person want to talk to Bernie Madoff or Osama Bin Laden. I keep up with the news on the ship's radio."

"Ah, since you've put me in such good company, I'll continue to chat. So why don't you have a passport? If you had one we could go down the pier and have lunch."

"I thank you for the invitation's thought. Ok. I came to Florida with my mother and sister when I was six years old. Then I tried to get back in to help my father get out. He had been injured. His leg was amputated. I was sixteen at the time. Stupid kid. Trusted the wrong people. I got caught. I spent three years in jail. My father died before I got out. Then I cut sugar cane. Then because I learned to sail in Florida, I got a job on a sailing vessel. Not this one. A bigger one. Then a few years ago I got this job. That was–" He had turned around as he spoke and saw the captain walking down the pier. "Jesus," he said, "you gotta get off the boat! My captain's back. Holy Shit!"

"Where can I go?" Lilyanne frantically asked. "There's only the water or the pier and he's coming down the pier!"

"Would you get wet for a stranger?"

"Good grief! What else can I do? Lower me over the side!" She grabbed her tote bag and went to the opposite side and Leonardo lowered her as gently as he could into the water.

He tossed a rope down to her. "Maybe he just forgot something."

He turned to see Captain Alejo Quintero looking up at the ship, waiting for him to put the boarding ladder over the side.

"Just a minute!" Leonardo said in Spanish. "I just left the head."

"Drinking too much juice?" Quintero asked as he climbed on deck, noticing the two plastic cups.

"I was thirsty. The boy came back here selling them. Did you forget something?"

"Yes. I had a small envelope that I hope I lost here and not on the way to the bank." He went down into the galley and found the envelope. "Got it!" he called. "Always something!" he groused and left the ship.

Leonardo Arenas pulled Lilyanne out of the water. "I am so sorry," he said. "You were so kind to me and I pay you back by tossing you 'in the drink.'"

Lilyanne remembered Sensei's admonishments. She had not acted in any way that was kind. She had deliberately bought him a pineapple drink because she was interested in the gun in his gun belt.

"Leonardo," she said, "you had to do what you did. To not do it would have gotten us both in trouble. I have no business being here. But I am, and I am soaking wet. I need to get dry."

"If you've got a cellphone in that bag, it's probably ruined," he said. "I feel terrible and I've got no way to replace it."

"It's my fault for being here. So don't worry about it. Fortunately, my passport's in a waterproof case. Do you have a shirt I could put on while I hang my skirt over one of the lines so that it dries. And my sandals, too. I'm lucky they stayed on my feet."

Leonardo went below and returned with a man's shirt. He turned away so that she could remove her dripping skirt and put his shirt on in private.

Seeing her sun hat start to float away, he got a long-poled boat hook and fished it out of the water. Because her hair was wet, he put the hat on his head. "Am I pretty?" he asked.

"Gorgeous."

In half an hour her skirt and hat were dry. She returned his shirt and put her skirt and hat on. "It's time for me to go," she said. "Even with the salt-water bath, I had a very nice time. Can I visit you tomorrow?"

"I hope you do," he said.

As she walked down the pier she realized that her hands had not trembled once in the last couple of hours.

At the Lamark Hotel she ordered a full course meal from room-service and when it arrived she asked the waiter, "Tell me, do you know what a Remittance Man is?"

"Ah yes, Ma'am," he said. "The Caymans are full of 'em, from just about every country in the world. And the funny thing is, while we don't know why they got kicked out of their own houses, when they come here they ain't no trouble at all. None at all. Just nice guys... and some gals, too. I guess you call them Remittance Gals." He laughed.

Lily laughed too, but the waiter's little joke deflated her swelling hope that she had found her quarry. How sure was she the day that she thought she saw Eric Haffner? She had never seen him out of his chauffeur's uniform. And the glimpses she had gotten of him in the photographs were of a man disguised. And his friend who liked boys? That really didn't sound like Henri now that she thought about it. She signed the check and said, "Mmmm" as she surveyed the food. But the moment the waiter closed the door and she was alone in the room, she pushed her chair away from the table. She no longer wanted to eat. She wanted to talk to Sensei but she knew she had no right to do that. She was not to talk to him again until she had an answer to his question.

She had told herself that she had traveled to the Cayman Islands to weigh the "possibilities" - that margin of change; but this, too, she had begun to doubt.

She walked to the window and looked out over the island and at the nearby sea. She was in the westernmost part of the Islands and her window faced west. A mellowing sun shone upon the many boats that were coming to the harbor for the dinner hour. She thought about Leonardo and wished she could see him again without compromise... just spend an evening with him... talking. But it wouldn't end with conversation. She knew enough to know that much.

She recalled the photographs of Martin Williams and his wife. She picked up the telephone directory. There were dozens of listings for the name "Williams." She sighed. "And I thought 'Smith' was bad," she mumbled. There were two Martin Williams listed. She called the first one and spoke to a man with a cockney accent who didn't know what the

Christian Eleemosynary Action group was or meant. The second one was answered by a recording. In a Jamaican lilt, a woman's voice answered, "Ya'v reached da office of Mah'in Williams an I'm happy ta say that he's doin' bettah. He says he reads all ya' caads and he smells each one uh'da flawahs ya be senden. He's gonna be back witcha all and very soon." She put the telephone book away.

As she went into the bathroom to run the bath water, she saw herself in the mirror. "My God!" she exclaimed. "I look emaciated!" She turned and went back to the dining table. "What would George say if he saw me looking like this? He'd sit me down and make me eat."

She cut and ate the prime rib before it had a chance to get any colder.

There is nothing unusual about the loosening of bonds that for many years held a group of individuals together. However much they shared a common purpose and worked well to achieve it, the potency of their attraction, like a compounded medication, seems to have an "expiration date" beyond which their association serves no discernible use.

The members do not become inert at the same rate. Some, more delicately formulated, disintegrate more quickly. But over all, the cause of the "shelf life's" termination is simply time. The adage: "I am not the same person I was when I was seventeen, but neither am I anybody else," reminds them all that, in one way or another, they, as individuals, have changed. That valence, so critical to their function as a unit, has only an historical significance, a sentiment that is barely appreciated in their now weakened versions of their elemental selves.

Eric Haffner was the first of the "four swindlers" to realize that the group no longer functioned cohesively. He welcomed the new independence. In 2010 he bought an abandoned mine and its buildings on Cayman Brac. He wanted to devote his time to renovating the main building, and though he did not explicitly announce his intention to settle down, he inspected the rooms that could be used as bedrooms and decided which would make the best nursery.

The structure, an eleven-room office and residence, had a square box-shape. In consideration of the hurricanes that occasionally struck the island, beauty had been sacrificed to strength. Eric recognized the building's potential to be esthetically pleasing - it would take little in the way of renovation to soften contours and enliven the drab grey of its exterior. But when he enthusiastically showed it to Charlotte La Fontaine, she dismissed it haughtily. It was, she insisted, like the 9 to 5 habitat of bureaucrats. "A man with your taste would never consent to live in a place like this." The other two members of the group concurred. Charlotte's son, Henri La Fontaine, thought it looked like a "fort without a tower," and Martin Shannon Williams suggested, "bars on the windows would add a delightful touch."

At first, Eric was offended; and then he became resentful. As he continued to renovate the building, he frequently sailed to George Town to buy supplies, but he did not contact any of the group while he was in town. He would stay overnight in his own small apartment and buy whatever he needed and then sail back to "the Brac." Yet, when Charlotte, to whom he had been closest, wanted to speak to him, he was polite and as cooperative as he thought it was in his best interest to be.

In August of 2011 Charlotte called a "meeting of the board." Decisions had to be made. Eric sailed to George Town and went to the Williams' house to discuss the dissolution of the Christian Eleemosynary Actions, Ltd. - their phony "African Mission" charity - and the Barracuda Supply Company - their business which sold imaginary supplies to the non-existent missions; and also to arrange for the sale of the Williams' house which had been purchased with common funds.

Because they had so cleverly established themselves in fictitious identities, the Cayman Islands had been a safe and pleasant haven for them. The charity scam that they operated enabled them to live well and to pay for the maintenance of legitimate properties they owned elsewhere. Whenever she was in George Town (and not tending to the non-existent flocks of needy Africans) Charlotte used two other identities: mostly she called herself Harriet Williams, the wife of Martin Williams, who shared with her husband the position of resident agent of the Christian Eleemosynary Actions, Ltd.

But to travel to and from the Caymans from Europe or from any of the locations in which they conducted their scams, she used the name, passport and pilot's license of the fictitious Beatrix van Aken, who was the mother of Claus and Willem van Aken, the two young blonde men who owned and operated the Barracuda Supply company. Charlotte always preferred to have an escape hatch available, and Beatrix van Aken's identity functioned well as this portal.

Charlotte La Fontaine opened the meeting by announcing, "The engagement and blackmail scam has run its course." Everyone nodded in agreement. She continued, "I for one think that it's time we repaired to our separate homes." This also created no dissension. It was not until Eric learned how "separate" the properties had become at the time of the dissolution, that he began to feel abused. He had spent his own money buying and renovating the mining property, but suddenly the proceeds from the Williams' house, the purchase and maintenance costs of which had been deducted from their common income, would go exclusively to Martin Williams. Eric stared at Charlotte when she said, "I'll go home to my estate in the Alpine foothills; Henri will return to our family home in Martinique; Eric will go to his new place on Cayman Brac; and Martin and Henri, being lovers, will live on Martinique or on Martin's yacht - both places that are extremely expensive to maintain. To live by minimal standards, they'll require more cash. I'm proposing that all of the proceeds of the Williams house go to Martin." And then she added, "But before anyone can live anywhere else, repairs have to be made to the houses in France and Martinique."

"Am I to understand," Eric countered, "that you intend to use company money to repair your houses? I'd like to remind you that you, Henri, and Martin have lived in the Williams' house at company expense. I rented my own small apartment out of my own money. And I just bought a property that I am renovating at my own expense, yet you want to use company funds to renovate yours. This is patently unfair - as is the donation of my quarter interest in the Williams house to Martin."

Charlotte tried to explain. "The house in France has an income from tenant farmers; but the Martinique residence is nothing but expense.

Both houses require a staff of year-round servants. Over the years we've all enjoyed living in both properties. Martin's ketch and Henri's house are expensive to maintain. Henri and I both think that financial worries have dampened Martin's enthusiasm for moving to Martinique. I can restore your 25% if you feel that strongly about it, but they can have my quarter interest."

Martin had a remedy. He proposed that they give the "diamond mine" scam another workout. He owned a worthless piece of land in Angola that he referred to as his "*fazenda*" which served as the location of an imaginary diamond mine. "I'll go to Angola and have the usual photos taken with various leaders and then we'll prepare a luscious brochure featuring my contacts and of course the operation of some prosperous diamond mine. If you three agree to shill for me when I sell shares in the mine, then from whatever we earn we'll first reimburse Eric for what he's already spent buying the property on the Brac; and then, since he has so much more work he wants to do, pay equally for the costs of the repairs to all three properties. I'll also guarantee him 25% of what we earn from the sale of the Williams house. How does that sound? Henri and I can live nicely on what we earn from the con."

It sounded fine to Eric. It was therefore tentatively decided that Eric Haffner would live in his new home on Cayman Brac and that he would live there under his Cayman Islands name: Claus van Aken. Henri La Fontaine would cease pretending to be Claus's brother, Willem van Aken, and as himself he would move into his family home on Martinique. Martin would also move into the house on Martinique with Henri, his long and adoring lover, and he and Henri would also spend as much time as possible sailing on Martin's beautiful ketch, *Sesame*. And Charlotte La Fontaine would return to her estate in the Alpine foothills. She might even take an apartment in Paris.

Everyone would remain "good friends."

Eric announced, "The lease on my apartment and on the Barracuda Supply Office will both expire on the last day of February, 2012. We have six months to wind down our business. Until then, I'll pay my own apartment rent and the company can pay for the supply company's office."

25

Everyone agreed that this arrangement was equitable.

After the meeting, Charlotte spoke to Eric alone. "Darling," she said, "I've got to talk to you in private about what is really on my mind." They walked to the beach and sat on the sand before she told him the real purpose of the company's dissolution. "I know that I brought Martin into our home and never objected to the relationship between Henri and Martin. But over the years Henri has become more effeminate and acts as though he would be content to live out his life with Martin. Henri has his father's title to honor and pass along to his children. It is no trivial matter to be the Conte deLisle. How can he do that attached to Martin? He has met and gone through the 'courtship' process with many qualified young women. Before he loses his ability to marry and have children, he needs to take seriously this noble burden."

Eric personally did not consider being a deLisle anything but a noble amusement. The family was never the stuff of statesmen. He asked, "Is this what was behind that generous payout to Martin? Are you trying to give him more money to make him more independent? How am I supposed to help that situation? I'm not gay. I don't travel in their circle of friends."

"If Henri expresses any desire to accompany Martin to Africa for the diamond mine scam, please try to discourage him. On the other hand, encourage him to enter society in Martinique. You might even consider spending a week or so with him there. Many wonderful families with marriageable daughters live on the island. While Martin is away, I'm hoping that between the two of us, we can talk Henri into at least going through the motions of courtship and marriage. In short, Eric, I want and need grandchildren... two, anyway."

"Martin seems to have cooled off about you, me, Henri, and Martinique," Eric noted. "He's restless."

"I've noticed it, too. I haven't mentioned this before, but I can see it clearly in his increasing indifference to Henri and in the cavalier way he speaks to him. I'm suspicious of his sudden revival of the diamond mine scam. He has a fascination with African boys. Ah, well... with God's help Martin will find somebody else, and though Henri's heart will be broken, he'll survive."

Eric agreed to do what he could. "Let's just get the Angola scam going. I want to put an end to this kind of life. We have until the end of February 2012."

They moved forward with the plans. In August 2011, the CEA, Ltd. was legally dissolved. Martin went to Angola to get the diamond mine scam started by having himself photographed with various leaders. Henri left for Martinique to attend to the renovations of the family house. Charlotte stayed in George Town to oversee cosmetic renovations to the Williams' property to prepare it for sale. Eric, using the name Claus van Aken, returned to Cayman Brac to continue working on the renovations of his property.

Then, in October, 2011, Martin became infected with AIDS and several other sexually transmitted diseases. He quietly entered a hospital in Kingston, Jamaica for treatment. The doctors were able to cure everything except AIDS; but they did start him on a successful anti-retroviral cocktail of four pills three times a day. Charlotte, as his "wife" went to Kingston in November to bring him home to the Caymans. She was appalled by what she encountered. He weighed half as much and had aged twice as much.

She hoped that Henri would be revolted by Martin's appearance. Instead, to her horror, Henri returned immediately from Martinique in order to fret and flutter over "his patient." Now, not only did she face the difficulty of getting Henri to the altar, but there was the distinct possibility that he would contract the disease and end his reproductive ability completely.

After his initial positive response to the anti-retroviral cocktail, Martin's health faltered. He suspected that his prescription was not properly being filled and blamed the druggist for giving him inferior or expired drugs. Charlotte obliged him by taking his prescription to another pharmacy; but his condition continued to deteriorate. She was certain that however much he might suspect her of tampering with the pills, he had never actually seen her destroy the contents of two of the four capsules he was to receive three times a day. She had always been extremely careful.

Henri wanted to take Martin to Paris for further consultation, but Charlotte so enthusiastically pretended to favor this idea, that Martin, irritable and suspicious, refused to go. Unfortunately, he had a distant cousin who lived on Grand Cayman Island, and in a fit of pique he went to live with him (as a paying guest) and his condition immediately improved. Afraid of being cheated by the other three during the sale, he quickly returned to the Williams house.

With help only from day laborers he found near the island's tourist attractions, Eric restored the house, converting what had been a well-built battleship grey cinderblock building into a stuccoed cozy single-storey ranch house. By the winter of 2011 he had completed the remodeling and was beginning to furnish the rooms.

Other than a generator which he rarely used, he delighted in the fact that he had no electricity. He loved to sit in his own living room and read by lamplight. He needed a woman... not any woman... but a woman of quality - educated and well-bred. They would have children. Yes, two boys and two girls. What would their last names be? Haffner or van Aken? Getting a proper woman and solving the problems of the care and feeding of his offspring - these were the problems that occupied Eric Haffner's mind. A clean, well-ordered life. A family man. A force for goodness and progress. Since he couldn't discard or repair his criminal past, he chose to ignore it.

Trouble began when Martin, embittered by having contracted diseases from persons he had regarded as friends, became aggressively intolerant of Charlotte's imperial manner. If she had not been so difficult to live with, he reasoned, he would not have gone back to Africa and acted recklessly to spite her. Ultimately, she was to blame for his illness. His congenial personality vanished and in its place was an irascible old and moody crank. He disliked and distrusted everyone around him and longed to return to a new young lover he had found in Namibia.

Charlotte feared that prejudice against the disease would deter some people from purchasing the place. "Your skin hangs on you. People will ask, 'Who is that emaciated fellow who lays around the living room or the lanai?' And they will be told that it is a well-known AIDS patient. Do you think they'll want their children crawling all over a toilet you've been using?" The real estate agent agreed that Martin's presence would not be a "selling point" when presenting the house.

Since his cousin lived too far away for quick transportation to and from his home, Martin had to find a more convenient place to stay whenever the real estate agent was going to show the property. Charlotte decided that he could use either Eric's apartment or the storage room of the Barracuda Supply Company office. These places would be available only until the end of February 2012, but she expected to conclude the sale by then.

If, however, the sale was not concluded by then, she decided that everyone would sail up to Cayman Brac and stay at Eric's place and use island air transportation for business meetings. Eric did not welcome this prospect, but she knew that if he wanted his quarter share of the house's proceeds, he would have to agree to the arrangement.

Eric, however, put a limit on his hospitality. On his property there was an assayer's laboratory which he had not renovated since he used the building as a maintenance and storage shed. He swept out the laboratory, cleaned its windows, pushed all the left-over chemical supplies to the back of the shelves and workbench, and put all the glassware and small appliances into a cabinet's drawers. Eric's vision of a clean well-ordered home that was filled with healthy children did not include persons of grandfatherly age who suddenly contracted an array of sexually transmitted diseases. He scrubbed down an old miner's cot that had been left in the main building and put it in the laboratory for Martin's use.

SATURDAY, FEBRUARY 18, 2012

Lilyanne ate a large breakfast and ordered a special fruit plate, pastries, and large containers of coffee to go.

Because she didn't want the coffee to cool, she took a cab to the dock and hurried out to the Santiago. If Leonardo wanted to eat down in the galley, it would be safe, she reasoned, to be alone with him in the morning.

"I've just about given up," she said, telling him about the waiter's comments. "I really didn't get that good a look at the owner of the Remittman. I mean... I was maybe 10 yards away from him. It looked like him, but I wouldn't bet my life on it. Blonde men of about thirty-five who are trim and athletic all look pretty much the same when you think about it."

Leonardo put his hands on her waist and lifted her up to sit her on a boom's furled sail. "You're too thin."

"I know. I've made up my mind to regain a lot of weight that I recently lost. I just ate breakfast, so you'll have to eat this food alone. But I'll drink some coffee with you."

Leonardo Arenas was grateful for the breakfast. "I don't get baked goods of this quality any more. Beans and rice. I think if we Cubans go to hell we won't find flames. Our punishment will be to have to walk through a gummy mass of beans and rice... burned on the bottom. Are you sure you don't want any of this pastry? Because if you don't, I'm gonna eat it all."

"Be my guest," she said, enjoying the sea breeze that blew her hair in all directions. But soon the wind picked up and Arenas suggested they sit in the galley.

She followed him into the cabin. He showed her the four bunks. Three had blankets and pillows, the fourth, a top bunk, contained mostly books and newly laundered shirts and jeans.

"I sleep in that one," he pointed to the bunk beneath the "shelf" bunk. "The head is up front... forward."

They sat at the table in the galley and for an hour they sipped coffee and talked about their lives and the condition of the world. She asked, "When are you heading back to Cuba?"

"Tomorrow morning. We got a late start this trip."

"Do you have anyone at home waiting for you?"

"Yes... I have a family." He took out a photograph of his wife and two children. "My mother has seen my children only in photos. She blames herself for putting me in jeopardy. But life goes on. I'm not bitter about it. I've got a good woman and smart kids."

When they finished eating, they worked together to clean up. Lilyanne took a bottle of spray cleaner and wiped the table with paper towels. Leonardo laughed. "Should I take the trash out, dear?" he joked as he pushed the empty coffee cups and pastry box down into the Trash Trapper.

"Leo!" Captain Quintero suddenly called from the dock. "*La escalera!*"

"Jesus!" Arenas whispered, looking around frantically. "Get inside that top bunk and cover yourself up!" He hoisted her up and as she wiggled herself down behind the books and laundry, he tossed his blanket and her tote bag up to her.

Quintero was angry. "The ladder!" he snarled again.

"I was in the head," Leonardo protested, hooking the boarding ladder over the side. The captain climbed up and went directly to the wheelhouse and started the little engine. "Cast off," he shouted.

"Aye," said the first mate who untied the line, tossed it to Leonardo, and jumped up onto the ladder as the motor dropped out of idle into gear.

Lilyanne knew that they were moving. She had heard the command to cast off, but she doubted that it could have meant to leave the Island. It had all happened too fast.

She lay in the bunk and tried not to panic. Fortunately she had her tote bag with her. Maybe they were just moving the vessel, she thought, putting it into a slip instead of letting it lie full length against the pier. But then she heard a sail snap and she could feel the ship pitch as the wind caught the sail. "Dear God," she said, "we're underway. What have I done? Leonardo will be reprimanded and it's all my fault!"

She waited for Leonardo to admit to the captain that she was on board. She would hear his apology, and she'd be able to hear or to guess what excuse he had given. He would definitely let her know what to say. George Town was at the front end of a long island. They could drop her off at any place along the long shoreline. She'd pay them for their trouble. She had come on board uninvited, after all. How was Leonardo supposed to reject the food she had brought?

An hour passed and her panic became claustrophobic under the blanket. She considered just climbing down and facing the captain; but she feared so many possible consequences - Leonardo's punishment... her being thrown overboard... a Cuban jail... becoming a maritime sex-slave. Her courage failed her and she decided to stay hidden.

Every day, the three men rotated through six four-hour shifts or "watches" at the wheel. The ship's bell would be rung once at the end of a watch to alert the next man to come to the wheel. The first watch began at 8 p.m. and since it was impossible to keep Lilyanne hidden in the bunk any longer, Leonardo picked that time to let the captain know that he had a "passenger" on board. The captain, he reasoned, would have calmed down by then and mundane things had a way of being diminished in importance when the night sky was in full view.

As Captain Quintero rang the bell that summoned him to the wheel, Leonardo addressed him as "Señor," and said that he had to confess something terrible that he had done. He spoke softly and related how the "accident" had occurred and how he thought the captain had merely forgotten something and would leave immediately and then, since the girl was already preparing to leave the ship, he'd just let her continue on her way. Words could not express his shame and regret about this error.

"¿Qué? ¿Está a bordo ahora?"

Well, he had to admit, she was. The captain summoned the first mate and ordered him to take the wheel. The two men proceeded to the cabin and Leonardo told Lilyanne to get up and come into the galley to speak to the captain.

"Not before I go to the bathroom!" she snapped. "How much longer did you think I could wait?" She lowered herself down and reached back to get her tote bag. Quintero, expecting a wharf whore, was surprised by her appearance. He stood in her way. "Move!" she shouted and marched forward to the head.

"*¿Estás demente?* he asked Leonardo. His face and voice registered shock and disbelief. Rules had been broken and the consequences were - none of them - good. Leonardo tried to minimize the damage. "She's just a girl who brought me some breakfast. You came back early and surprised us. She was just in a hurry to get to the head," he explained. "She's been up in the bunk all afternoon," Leonardo shrugged. "She just has to go to the bathroom."

Lilyanne returned to the galley and sat at the table. Quintero, so furious that he forgot ninety percent of the English he knew - which, normally, he could speak very well - was reduced to asking Leonardo Arenas to translate.

He made her sit directly across from him in the galley. He could see the colorful paper containers in the trash and knew that a wharf whore would not have come with expensive hotel take-out. "Are you some kind of spy?" he managed to ask.

"No," she said. "I just brought Leonardo breakfast. He was helpful to me yesterday. He gave me good advice about locating someone I was looking for. I wanted to thank him."

"Give me your phone."

She handed him her dead phone. He pushed a few buttons. "And you're not a spy? You didn't destroy the phone so that I couldn't get the numbers? What do you take me for?"

"I'm not a spy."

"What are you? Why are you here? Who hired you?"

"I'm not anything. I was looking for someone, that's all."

He opened her passport case. "A woman in her twenties who is not anything. I think you need to do better than that. You went to school. You studied to be something. What are you if not a spy?"

"I used to be a postulant. I was less than a year away from taking my final vows as a nun."

"I ought to slap your face for that lie. My mother was a good Catholic. She loved God and the Virgin and Jesus and all that stuff. Your lie makes a mockery of her life. They call whores 'nuns' in some countries. Is that what you are? Some kind of spy whore?"

Lilyanne was offended. "I was in a convent for five years. Test me if you know so much about Catholicism."

Quintero laughed malevolently. "Recite the *Hail Mary*."

"Which language would you like? English, Latin, Spanish, French or German?"

"All of them, *Puta!*"

Lilyanne made the Sign of the Cross and without hurrying her recitation, she began to pray aloud. First, she began in Latin: *"Ave Maria, gratia plena, Dominus tecum, benedicta tu in mulierbus..."* She finished the prayer and immediately began the Spanish. *"Dios te salve, Maria, llena eres gracia, el Señor es contigo..."* Her eyes remained downcast and if Quintero intended his expression to tell her to stop, his intention was frustrated. As she continued to recite all the prayers his face grew redder and his facial muscles contracted so strongly that he looked as though he would soon explode. He was breathing furiously as she finished. Then he slammed both hands down on the table, got up and left the cabin, shouting something to Leonardo who followed him. Lilyanne caught a few of the words... *carcel... autoridades cubanas... polizon...* "Dear Lord," she said, "They're gonna turn me in as a stowaway or a spy or something!"

The captain's jacket hung on a hook in the galley. A cellphone... possibly a satellite cellphone... was sticking out of the pocket. If only she could get to it she could call for help. Quintero returned to the galley. "Get back up there in the bunk!" he ordered. She picked up her tote bag and tried to climb up into the shelf-bunk. As Quintero tried to help her, he noticed the scars of an old burn injury to her foot; and he began to curse himself and the world.

SUNDAY, FEBRUARY 19, 2012

Since Lilyanne had been discovered, she had not been permitted to be alone. She could see the captain's jacket and the cellphone in its pocket, but she had had no opportunity to use it. Although Quintero did not speak to her at all, she did notice that all three men were becoming increasingly relaxed around her. She decided that the next time the captain went to relieve Hugo at the wheel, she would access the phone whether Leonardo objected or not. With any luck, he would be sleeping.

It was not until Sunday evening, at 8 p.m., when Leonardo went to relieve the captain for First Watch and Hugo stayed on deck and the three of them talked - she could not tell what they were saying - that she jumped down from her bunk, grabbed the cellphone and called the only number she could think of calling that followed the prefix 1-215.

George was in the shower when his phone rang the first time. He did not hear the ring. Lilyanne agonized through the interminable instructions on how to leave a voice mail message and what to do if she wanted more options and whispered finally, "George... I'm in bad trouble... I need you. Help me—" and then, hearing one of the men coming across the deck towards the cabin, she disconnected the call. She pushed the cellphone back into Quintero's jacket and scrambled to her bunk bed, pretending that she was trying to get down to go to the head.

"I thought I was supposed to be guarded," she said, pretending annoyance. "I have to go to the bathroom and nobody was here to walk me up there."

George finished his shower and was rubbing the towel against his wet hair when he thought he heard the phone ring. He went into his kitchen, glanced down at the caller and, seeing that it was a rug and drapery cleaning service call, he chose to let it go to voice mail. He put on pajamas, flicked on the TV, and selected a movie to watch.

MONDAY, FEBRUARY 20, 2012

Lily had lain awake in the cabin's total darkness, listening to Hugo's gentle snoring while Leonardo took First Watch. Finally, she heard the bell ring. Hugo awakened, yawned, and made his way aft. It must be midnight, she thought. She had not heard Captain Quintero make any sleeping noises and didn't know if he was in the cabin at all. In a few minutes Leo came into the cabin, sat on his bunk, kicked off his shoes, and stretched out. In another few minutes she could hear him breathing rhythmically.

What snips of conversation she had overheard and understood did not promise a pleasant future for her. They were approaching Cuban waters. She was tired and weak and her nerves had taken all that they could take of her imprisonment in a rolling ship's bunk. It took all the fortitude she had left to keep from crying. "I am on a mission and if it takes a hundred years, I'm not going to do anything else," she told herself. "Anything else" evidently included sleeping.

She wanted to go up on deck. She knew that she had agreed to stay in her bunk; but the frustration of being unable to sleep had worn down her promise to its inconsequential nub. Maybe, she thought, sitting on deck she'd fall asleep. She carefully put her legs over the side of the bunk and lowered herself to the floor. Then, holding onto anything that would keep her from toppling over, she made her way aft until she was standing under the starlit sky.

"Hi Hugo," she said meekly. "There's no moon tonight."

"Sí. It's New Moon tomorrow. No moon tonight. It's good we don't have to navigate by the stars anymore. We might wind up in Key West."

"That's progress for you," she said in a gentle but serious voice, "One step forward, two steps back."

"For you, maybe."

"What is the Captain going to do with me?"

"Nothing. What can he do? You are the problem of the Cuban Authorities, not him."

"You know that technically I'm really not a stowaway. I wasn't trying to get a free ride into Cuba."

Hugo laughed as if to say, *Nobody would want to get a free ride into Cuba.* "Señorita," he said, "I'm not going to touch that comment with a ten-foot pole." He giggled again then he cleared his throat. "Ah," he said, "you might want to go back to your bunk before the Captain sleepwalks and finds you out here. You don't need more trouble."

"I couldn't stay inside another minute. Let him be mad. He can't get any madder than he already is. Maybe I'll get lucky and he'll throw me overboard."

Captain Quintero emerged from the cabin fully awake. He had not been sleeping when she lowered herself from the bunk. He walked back to the wheel. "Aren't you supposed to be asleep?" he asked.

"I'm not supposed to be here at all," she said.

Quintero took the wheel. "Go below," he said to Hugo. "Get some sleep. You'll maybe have to be doing work for two soon. Come back for the first Dog Watch. I'll take it again from there."

"The larboard running light blinked a few times," Hugo said. "It can't need a new battery. I just put one in two days ago. Maybe there's a loose wire."

"Check it in the morning. It's steady now."

Lilyanne sat on the deck looking up at the stars. She turned her head around and saw all that she could see that was unobstructed by the sails. Then she crawled to the other side and crawled back. "You can't see anything at all over there," she said, bracing herself for an unpleasant response.

Instead, he said, "Do you know the constellations?"

"Most of them... the major ones, anyway. When I was in the convent my father sent me a computer program so that I could study the stars. We weren't allowed out after sundown so aside from a few planets, I never got to see them 'in the flesh' you might say... until I was put on kitchen duty in the winter. I'd have to get up extra early; and then I'd be able to peek when I took the garbage outside. But to see the whole sky? No, for five years I didn't see the whole sky... not like this anyway."

He tested her. "Can you see Orion?"

"Yes." She pointed to the three stars in the belt. "One, two, three. His belt is hard to miss."

He sighed. "Why did you do such a foolish thing and come on my boat?"

"Well, I didn't expect you back. Leonardo had been nice to me. I've been very nervous and depressed lately... mad at the world. I lost weight and couldn't sleep. He was nice to me and I brought him breakfast because, for some reason, I felt like eating after I met him. He's easy to talk to. Neither of us expected you to come back so soon."

"That is obvious. Why are you depressed?"

"I think it is called 'getting what I deserved for being a smart-ass.' It's a long story."

"I have time."

"All right, then. A bunch of swindlers... con men... used some kind of marriage enticement to lure rich unmarried girls into thinking they were engaged to this handsome young French nobleman - who, by the way, really does have a chateau in the eastern side of France. Then they would drug the girl and take obscene photographs of her and then an anonymous third party would work the blackmail and insist that as a penance for her immoral behavior donations to a charity would have to be made. The charity is or was based in George Town. They'd, in effect, sell the photos to the girl's father and the payoff money came down here. Then the engagement would be broken off, naturally. We couldn't have such a man of integrity connected to a woman who had those awful pictures taken of her! They did this to a girl in Seattle and then they moved on to another victim, in this case, me. She collapsed emotionally immediately. I didn't. I didn't understand Post Traumatic Stress Syndrome. I was full of good advice. She simply had to forgive him. Faith and prayer. I told her how I dealt with the catastrophe. I had all the answers. After she was finally cured, I began to have nightmares, loss of appetite, the shakes, heart palpitations. I got psychiatric treatment that didn't work. But I talked to a Zen priest and got some direction in my misery. I no longer follow the old unwise philosophy. I follow the new ethics. Well, almost. I'm not finished the course yet."

"Were you physically harmed... I mean... besides the sexual assault?"

"No. Ultimately I was rescued by a wonderful man, a private investigator named George Wagner. I was able to take refuge in his house. I was pretty sick from the drugs they gave me. He and his partner took me to the hospital. I was admitted overnight. It was awful."

"Leo says you were looking for a man who owed your father money, there on the docks. He mentioned the ship, the Remittman. I've seen that guy. Is he the French nobleman?"

"No, he played the part of the chauffeur."

Quintero chuckled thinking of the foolishness of worlds that contained such creatures as personal chauffeurs. "Chauffeur!" he laughed again. "How many were there?"

"Four. That guy was the chauffeur, Eric; and Henri, the lovesick courtier - he really had a title - my dad checked him out; and his mother Charlotte, Le Contesse deLisle, who forced her son to break the engagement; and Martin, a big black guy who played the valet. I never actually met him. I mean... what would a respectable young woman be doing in the company of a gentleman's valet?" She laughed.

"It's good you can laugh about it. How much did it cost your father?"

"Two million in cash and another million in jewelry."

"What?" He whistled. "Senorita... don't you realize that by telling someone that your family has that kind of money you've made yourself a target for more thievery. I could hold you for ransom."

"You could. But seeing how precarious my present position is... Let's see. Door #1, get thrown over the side. Door #2, get sold into sex-slavery.

Door #3, spend half my life in a Cuban jail. Door #4, get ransomed by my father. I don't think telling you the truth is exactly to my disadvantage."

He laughed again. "Aii, chihuahua! I'm truly sorry that I cannot ransom you. Throw you over the side? Sell you into sex-slavery? No, none of these. But you don't want to spend a few years in a Cuban jail? What is wrong with you? It would be a holiday after Eric, and Henri... and who were the others?"

"Charlotte and Martin."

"Which would you prefer? A year with them or a year in a Cuban jail."

"Who am I going to kill in a Cuban jail?"

Quintero thought a moment. "Ah... So that is it! You came down to the docks to look for that Remittman. And what? Did you see Leonardo with a gun in its holster?"

"Exactly. The gun was the first thing I saw."

"Don't tell Leonardo. He thinks you were attracted to his handsome face. He's young."

They talked quietly about politics and astronomy and about sailing ships and the high cost of fuel that may make sailing ships come back into vogue. And then he returned to the topic of ethics, of forgiveness versus punishment.

"So," he asked, "your new ethics will allow you to shoot the chauffeur?"

"He did considerably more than drive me around... although I was unconscious at the time."

"And now you can't sleep and you lost your appetite and even when you're sitting still your heart can start beating like you're running for your life. I know the feeling. Some nights I lie in my bed and curse my clock or my watch... whatever is reminding me of the time."

"Turn about is fair play. Tell me why you're so miserable."

"And then have you blackmail me when you're in a Cuban jail by threatening to tell everyone my secrets?" He began to laugh again, in a warm, good natured way.

"You could ransom me if I try to blackmail you. You'll have time to do it. Go ahead, then. Keep it all inside you while it festers and swells up until you burst with a heart attack."

"That will solve my problem. Death solves everyone's problems."

"That's baloney! A person's death may destroy dozens of innocent people."

"Go into the galley and bring us a couple of beers. There's a little refrigerator under the table."

She went down into the cabin and got one bottle of beer from the refrigerator. As she handed it to him he said, "Put it in the net bag and take the wheel. I'm going to the head. Just keep her steady on course." He looked around to be sure there were no other ships' lights to be seen. "Just hold her on course." In a few minutes he returned. "Have you got Tahiti in sight?"

"Land, Ho," she giggled. "How's your French?"

He drank some of the beer and took the wheel. "So the advice to forgive and forget... that didn't work out as well as you thought it would?"

"No. I didn't understand the illness, so I couldn't remedy it."

"Now you want revenge?"

"No. Absolutely not. I'm not seeking justice for myself. It's a long and complicated story. I'd have to teach you the little bit of Zen that I learned. Is this your way of deflecting the question of your own misery?"

"Yes. I'm trying. Well, what the hell. It isn't as if my problem is a secret. Unfortunately, it is now common knowledge throughout my country. I've got five kids. The youngest one went bad and is in jail. My wife and I raised them all well. I had a relatively high rank in government so they weren't deprived of anything. Four of them went to graduate school. He, my youngest, his name is Francisco, wanted to become a doctor; but he wasn't able even to graduate from college. He didn't have the brains of the others. He got a job with the food distribution system... the old rationing system. He worked for the meat distribution department as a butcher for the Liberta Carnicero market. He got married and had a boy.

"His wife had a dog she loved. Her father gave it to her for her birthday... a bichon habenera... a valuable dog. When it was a few months old, her father was killed in a car accident. She went crazy with grief and she got it into her head that the dog was her father's 'familiar' - do you know what a 'familiar' is?"

"Yes, like the cat of a witch. The person puts his spirit into the animal for safe keeping."

"So she re-named that dog Padre, after her father. It was a Santeria kind of belief and we all figured she'd get over it. One day the dog got sick and was very weak. He needed meat. A dog is a dog. They were all wolves at one time. So my boy brings home some scraps of meat for the dog. Then it is more than scraps. Then my mother wants to make soup like she made in the old days for a fiesta. Vegetable beef soup. She grows vegetables in her little garden and has the carrots, peas, string beans, cabbage, and whatever else she puts in that soup. She asks Francisco to bring home a little meat for the broth. Soon he is stealing meat every night. His friends, his wife, her family, not to mention her father - the dog. He wanted to be an important man. Everybody loved him. Big man. I don't know what got into him. What was he thinking? Then the government switches from the old system to a new one and the theft is discovered. To hear the charges, he must have been stealing a side of beef every week. I guess every shortage was blamed on him. Now he's in jail. My family is disgraced. To steal food from children to give to a dog is a terrible crime... in *any* country. How could he think that he was entitled to help himself to meat that in our system really does belong to others. It was the worst kind of theft. I gave up my position in the government. I couldn't look my coworkers and friends in the eye. When this opportunity to sail came up, I took it. I rather be away from all that humiliation. At least on the sea all I have to worry about is a rich ex-nun stowaway."

"So you're grief-stricken over this crime?"

"Yes. To steal meat from children and give it to a dog? How would you react? You'll tell me to forgive him... that all men are sinners. I don't want to hear that. I can't forgive such stupidity and such selfishness in my own son."

"In my old ethical system, I would have told you to forgive him. But not in my new ethical system. For that advice, I'd have to ask a few questions first."

"What questions?"

"Did you enjoy the soup?"

"What?" Quintero's jaw clenched. The old rage surfaced. "What did you ask me?"

"I'll try another question. How many of the people who ate the meat volunteered to serve part of his jail sentence?"

Quintero did not answer. His breathing quickened.

"All right. Let me ask another question. Maybe it is not a crime to be a receiver of stolen goods in Cuba, so I'm not sure about this. Were you, your mother, his wife, and all the others charged with receiving stolen goods? You all knew that he was stealing meat but you ate it anyway. Is there a price you had to pay for that?"

The captain spoke to her as he had spoken the first day. "Nobody knew the extent of his theft! We did not sit around discussing meat. My mother wanted a little something for broth. A bone would have done the job. Yes, he brought meat, but it was for a celebration. He was going to eat the soup too, and he could easily have used his own rations to get it. His wife wanted a few scraps for a sick animal. The scraps would have been thrown away. Nobody knew the extent of his thievery."

"Señor... please! You tell me he was not as smart as the others. Don't tell me that they asked him to steal because they thought he was stupid enough to take the whole blame on himself if he got caught. If that's the kind of people they are, the wrong people are in jail. Don't delude yourself. You knew. You all knew. You patted him on the back and made him feel loved, and that's what encouraged him to steal. Hah! You ate the meat he stole, and now you despise him for being a thief. Why are you so enraged? Why can't you sleep? Because you know he is in jail... maybe being abused by vicious criminals, and all he did was want you to love him despite his being so stupid that he couldn't get through school. And he will suffer years of abuse while you delude yourselves into being so innocent and so ashamed of what he did.

"Señor, you need to go to the jail and ask *him* to forgive *you*. Then you'll sleep again. That's my new philosophical system talking."

Quintero's jaw was so clamped shut that he could barely say, "Go below, Señorita, or I *will* throw you over the side."

At 9 a.m. in his Germantown Avenue office, while he was up in the display window, looking over his 'needy' orchid plants, George's cellphone rang again. For a moment he thought he'd let voicemail get the call, but then he knew how Beryl would bitch and moan if he didn't pick up. He stepped down and went into his office and answered a routine business call. When he finished it, he checked his voice mail. He heard the words and was stunned. "George... I'm in bad trouble. I need you. Help me–"

If George had been struck by lightning while sitting in his office chair he would not have been so shocked as he was hearing Lilyanne's voice. Quickly, he hit the call back button, but the line crackled and hummed and then went dead. Again he tried and got no response. He did not know what to do. Beryl was still upstairs in her apartment. He took his phone and ran to the stairs.

"Ber! Ber!" he called, knocking loudly on her door.

Beryl was cleaning and opened the door holding a mop. "What's wrong?"

"Lilyanne's in some kind of trouble. I can't figure out what happened when she called and left a voicemail. When I listened she said, 'George, I'm in trouble. Big trouble. I need your help.' And then the call was disconnected, and when I tried to hit the 'call back' at first I got a lot of noise and then nothing and then I tried again and got zero. Nothing at all. Help me out, here! When it comes to her, I can never think straight."

"Go sit in the kitchen. I'll mop your footprints after you. My phone's in there."

He went into the kitchen and sat at the table watching with rising anger as she waved the mop back and forth over his footprints and her own. "Can't that wait?" he asked.

"No." She put the mop in the bucket and sat at the table. She flicked through her iPhone. "Who do we know at the telephone company? Hmmm." She found the number and called it.

"Jerry? This is Beryl. Can you talk? I know it's early."

Jerry Tannenbaum said he was technically on his coffee-break and could talk while eating a donut. "Shoot."

"Can you do a job for us? George just got a call from his... what should I call her... his 'angel girl' - are you and I on the same page with that?"

"Oh, yeah... the girl from the Main Line."

"Right. He got an emergency call from her... it came in last night and went to voicemail. Some twelve or thirteen hours later he got around to checking his voicemail and there it was. He hit the call back and the line first buzzed and hummed and then went sort of dead and then when he tried again it didn't do anything at all. Can you possibly trace the source of the call? I'll put him on the phone and if he can calm down enough to speak coherently, he'll give you the particulars." She handed her phone to George.

George furnished his number, the time the call came in and its duration. "Charge us anything you like. This is life and death stuff. Please hurry with the results, Jerry, as a favor to me. I mean, we'll pay you, but just hurry as a favor."

Beryl made breakfast as George waited in agony for Jerry Tannenbaum to call back with the information. Finally his phone's ring tone sounded and he answered it while the *"Nessun"* of *"Nessun Dorma"* was still playing. He spilled tea down the front of his shirt.

"Of all the gin joints in the world..." Jerry began, "your call had to come in from the black hole of communications... Cuba. It was made through CUBACEL via Intersputnik. That's right... Sputnik... Intersputnik. I'm not making this up. ETECSA - that's the Telecommunications Company of Cuba - controls all the country's telephone service and they are a black hole from which no light shineth. I can tell you that the international call prefix is 119. The country number is 53. If the phone call originated in Cuba on an ordinary cellphone, it would have been transmitted via Intersputnik. If it came in via landline it would have been transmitted via Intersputnik. If it originated outside that Island, by which I mean at sea, it would probably have been transmitted by Intersputnik whether or

not it was an ordinary cellular or a satellite phone. Although, especially at sea, they also use service provided by Caribbean Cellular C-COM., but this call, I think, came in on Intersputnik. But either way, the calls are still under the control of ETECSA. And ETECSA is not gonna tell you which number made the call."

Beryl got on the phone and asked what they owed him. He said, "nothing," but she knew that "nothing" doesn't get good service next time. "I'll send you a check for $500 which nowadays is nothing."

George paced through the kitchen. "What do I do now?" he asked.

"Call her father," Beryl suggested.

"You do it. I'm too nervous."

Beryl called and explained to Everett Smith the details of Lilyanne's call to George. Smith had no idea that Lilyanne had left the country. She had told him that she intended to visit Margaret Cioran in Seattle. "Cuba?" he exclaimed. "That makes no sense! She's been very nervous and has tried to keep to herself. I think she hasn't wanted to worry us. She had been in a Catholic clinic in Baltimore; but she didn't like the place and left after a few days. That was about three or four weeks ago, in January. Then she started to go out for long walks or drives. God knows where she went. She'd come home at night, tired... wouldn't eat much. She's lost weight."

"Did you give her cash or was she using credit cards for gas or other expenses?" Beryl asked.

"I didn't give her cash so I suppose she used her credit cards."

"Then you are going to have to use some muscle to get the credit card companies to tell you immediately what charges she made."

"I can handle that. All right, I'll call you right back."

Beryl went into the bathroom and took a shower. She was still in there when Smith called back and George answered the call.

"Sanford tells me," Everett said, "that he heard her make an appointment with Sensei Percy Wong. You might want to ask him why she wanted to see him."

George was speechless. His friend and colleague had not mentioned that he had seen her recently. He thanked Smith and said he'd ask him.

He shouted through Beryl's bathroom door. "You don't need makeup and your hair will dry in the temple! We need to talk to Perce!"

Sensei was adamant. "I'm sorry, George. I can't discuss her problems with you. Yes, she came to me for counseling and I gave her my counsel, such as it was. Lilyanne Smith's conversations with me are privileged."

George had never heard Sensei use such terms before. He did not understand. "Perce, she called me to come to her for help, but the call was disconnected. The call came in last night... voicemail. She said, 'George, I'm in big trouble. I need you. Help me.' I cannot call her back because she used a Cuban phone. Why did she come to you and not Beryl or me? What was the problem that took her to Cuba? *I need to know! You're supposed to be my friend. What is going on?*"

"Give me a break here, George. Before I'm anything else, I'm a Buddhist priest. When a person has a problem that he or she needs to talk to a priest about, that communication has to be inviolate. You have to appreciate the damage I can do to her if I betray her trust."

"This isn't some petty 'check-up on somebody' thing. Her life's in danger!" George's anxiety made him sound threatening. "*This is Lilyanne we're talking about and I need to be able to help her. Do you know why she'd be using a Cuban phone?*"

Beryl took control of the conversation. "George," she said quietly, "go outside and wait. I'll handle this." George growled and walked out of the temple kitchen. Beryl waited until he had shut the door before she continued to speak. "Look," she said gently, "he's obviously distressed and so was Lily when she called. I heard the message. Maybe the 'romantic love' angle is compromising you. If you're reluctant to talk to George about this, I can ask her father to talk to you; and if you still want to claim privilege, fine. We don't even know if her discussions with you are related to the trouble she's gotten herself into. She called for help on a Cuban phone and they don't give gringos information. So, again, do you happen to know why she'd be using a Cuban phone?"

"No. She never mentioned Cuba to me."

"Thanks, anyway. If you think of anything you can tell us that won't drop you into Mara's clutches, please let us know."

George was standing on the sidewalk. She took him by the sleeve, and walked him back to the office.

As they opened the front door, their office phone was ringing. Everett Smith was calling. "She charged a one-way airline ticket to George Town, Grand Cayman."

"Did she use it for a hotel?" Beryl asked.

"Yes, The Lamark. I called and she's still registered but she isn't in her room... that's room number 412."

"Tell him I'm on my way," George yelled. "If he hears anything at all, he's to call me immediately and I'll do the same."

Two hours later, George was sitting in first class - the only space he could get - on the next flight to George Town, Grand Cayman.

At George's request, the Lamark gave him Room 413, across from Lilyanne's room. Dinner was still being served in the dining room. Although he would have preferred to eat in his room, the likelihood that he would see Lilyanne in there was zero; and so he went down to the less formal of the hotel's two dining rooms and, sitting where he could get the best view of the entrance, he had his dinner. He had landed in George Town after eight o'clock in the evening on a Monday. He learned, to his surprise, that they were in the same time zone as Philadelphia.

There was nothing to do but watch people and then, after eating, to knock softly on Lily's door, and after getting no answer, to return to his room and try to think of why she would come to the Cayman Islands at all, at this time.

He picked up a phone book. There was no listing for the Christian Eleemosynary Action, Ltd. And there were no listings for any of the four old antagonists. He was too tired to think creatively. He needed to get some sleep.

TUESDAY, FEBRUARY 21, 2012

George woke up to the facts that it was Tuesday, that he was in George Town, and that he knew nothing about Lilyanne's reasons for being either in the Caymans or near Cuba on Sunday night.

The first order of business would be to check in with the local police to present his credentials. While he was there he would inquire about any unidentified bodies that had recently been recovered or whether a crime that involved the person he was seeking had been reported.

Chief Inspector Bruce Allan-Royce was friendly, British efficient, and sincerely desirous of helping to locate a missing tourist. George felt uneasy about being evasive but he certainly had not come to the Cayman Islands to help the police apprehend Lily if she had committed any crime while she was there. He thought he would give a second-tier truth: "I'll be honest. It's personal with me. I saw her through a very troublesome time in her life and you know how it is. You work so hard to save something that you just can't stand by and see it destroyed. Her father is my client. He's worried about her since she's the headstrong type and doesn't always listen to reason."

"Did you want to report her missing... formally?" the inspector asked.

"Not yet. I'll give you her name and my cellphone number and if anything comes up, I'd appreciate a call."

"We're an island and that means boats and I needn't tell you about maritime accidents. If an unidentified female turns up, I'll let you know."

George thanked him and felt relieved to have gotten that "touchy" check-in protocol over with. He returned to his hotel to see what he could learn through old-fashioned sleuthing.

He re-checked the internet for any activity of the Christian Eleemosynary Actions, Ltd. The old Public Relations' references had been taken down and there were no links whatsoever to any current activity in the Caymans or anywhere else on the planet.

He double-checked the telephone directory and saw what he already knew - that there were no listings for Charlotte and Henri La Fontaine, Eric Haffner, and Martin Shannon. The Christian Eleemosynary Action group which once did have a contact number was no longer listed. The registered agents for CEA, Ltd. were - he learned from his old notes - either Harriet or Martin Williams. There was no phone listing for Harriet Williams, but there were two for a Martin Williams. He called both numbers and got no answer from one and a recorded message from a Jamaican lady from the other. He put the book away.

He reasoned that the CEA had been registered within the last few years as a non-profit charitable group and, estimating the amount of money that had been transferred into its sacrosanct account, the principals surely were known. It wasn't such a big country that millions dropped into the account of a local citizen would pass unnoticed. Local. That was key. The CEA wasn't another one of those anonymous foreign entities. And if large amounts of money were put into their charity, they would be recognized for their philanthropy.

He made a list of people and places that could be sources of information. He could try the public library or a newspaper office. While there was no guarantee that either Harriet or Martin Williams was still in the Islands, if they owned property, the property tax records would have the listing. The Recorder's Office where deeds would have to be filed was also a possible source. But maybe ordinary folks knew them since their philanthropic works were so notable. He'd try the hotel desk first.

He dressed and went down to the lobby. Three women were behind the registration desk. The oldest-looking one was sorting papers of some kind. She looked bored. "Ma'am," he softly called.

She looked up. "Yes, can I help you?"

"I'm in Room 413. Everything's fine with my accommodations. You run a wonderful place and I'll be sure to mention it in my article. I wonder if you can give me a little direction. I'm writing a piece about the unsung heroes of the Caymans - in particular, about the good work that the Christian Eleemosynary Action folks do or, for years, did. I'm speaking of the Harriet and Martin Williams' group. When people give money to a charity, they like to know more about the folks who set such a good example for The Golden Rule. I don't want to start by approaching bureaucrats because, frankly, they always want to get their names or their departments mentioned. I just want to hear a few uplifting words about doing God's Work from the Williams' or from the folks who know them."

She teased him. "Are you going to tell me that if I tell you something nice about Harriet or Martin you won't mention my name?"

He laughed. "Bribery! This is bribery!" She giggled along with him.

He pointed to the telephone directory. "Is the CEA still in George Town? It's not in the book! Can they be doing their work under another name?"

"No... but you're too late. They've ended their work. The Good Lord saw fit to give Martin a disease that weakened him." She whispered, "AIDS from a bad blood transfusion. Ironic, isn't it? He went to one of the Missions they have there... I think it's one in Namibia... I'm not sure. But if you knew Martin Williams you'd understand. He's the kind of man who doesn't let someone just lie in the road. He gets out and helps the fella. And even if he's far from competent medical treatment, he'll risk his own health."

"The world needs more saints like him. Well... I don't want to burden him with posing for photographs or giving me an interview when it's his time to rest. What about Mrs. Williams? How is she holding up under this burden?"

"She's probably at home now at their place on Little Lake Drive. I don't think I'd go knocking there - you might disturb them. He seems to be better now, but she had her hands full taking care of him night and day. What you could do..." She reached into a desk drawer and withdrew stationery and an envelope. "Put your request in a note and leave it in their mailbox. It's got the hotel's phone number right on the letterhead.

Be sure to write your name clearly and your room number, too." She stood up and handed George the stationery.

"I'll do that," he read her name tag, "Ms. C. Carter. And just in case my article mentions it... is that C for Caring, or Cooperative, or Christian?"

"All three, I hope. A fourth guess would have been Connie." She sat down at her desk.

George leaned on the counter and looked into her eyes. "You are one of the nicest people I've met in a long time."

It struck him as odd, as he left the hotel, that he actually meant what he had said to her. He was still irritated by Sensei's refusal to give him any information. "And what does that say about my life?" he asked himself.

He left the hotel and hailed a cab. "Take me along Little Lake Drive. I want to see the houses there."

"Pretty street," said the driver.

They did not have to drive far before they came to the open, tree-lined street. George commented, "I like to see the houses from the streets... in the English and American style. In many Spanish styles all you see is a gate and a wall. If you want to see the house you have to get past the gate."

"Well, we're a territory of Great Britain. So if we look English, that's why."

"Yes, I see the Union Jack in your flag. You've got a beautiful country here. Well kept. Clean. Educated people. I wish the rest of the world were like this."

"We're lucky and we know it. I wouldn't live anyplace else... not if I could help it. If you like flowers, this is the place to be." He slowed down to point out a garden of riotous color. "The red flowers are *tower spirals;* the pink are *ishoras;* the orange are *corjas;* and we call those yellow flowers *buttercup cockleshells.*"

"They're all new to me. But I also see hibiscus and bougainvillea. Those I know. Tell me," George ventured, "do you know the Williams' residence?"

"Sure," he said. "It's up ahead a few blocks."

"I don't want to call on them. I was supposed to do an article on their philanthropical works, but I just learned that Mr. Wiliams got sick and they retired from missionary work. Is Mrs. Williams doing ok?"

"Yes, they're fine people."

"Is he finally recovered?"

"He's better. Out of the hospital. He used to be a big fella. Maybe 17 stone. That's like..." he calculated, "240 pounds. I guess because we got used to seein' him so big and strong, he seems so thin now. But if you didn't know he used to be like one of your Dallas Cowboys, he'd probably look like a normal guy... except for the saggin' skin. You'd never recognize him if all you got was old pictures." He slowed down and stopped at the curb. A sign said, "For Sale."

The house was set back at least fifty feet from the street. Someone was in the front yard, planting what seemed to be pansies. "There she is now," the cabbie said, "fixin' up the property for the real estate people."

"I won't bother her at a time like this," George said. He stared at the woman incredulously. He wished he could look through binoculars. He needed glasses to read and glasses to drive; and since he was doing neither, he had to get her into focus as best he could.

He remembered seeing her on the night of Lilyanne's engagement party: a regal woman in diamonds and sapphires and a white fox wrap with a blue gown trailing behind her as she stepped out of the limousine and then, with her right hand resting on top of Henri's hand, as she mounted the portico steps of Tarleton House. And there she was on her knees in a garden, planting flowers... with a hand spade and a watering can beside her. Her hair must have been rinsed brown. It was pulled severely back so that her ears completely showed. "Ah," George said, "keep drivin'. I don't want the dear lady to see us and think she's got to play hostess to company. That's what nice folks do when company calls. They drop everything." He looked around instinctively to see if there was a good place to mount a surveillance camera. He might decide to watch the house to see if Lilyanne was being held inside. There was a lamp post that would provide a perfect mounting for a surveillance camera. He made a note of the house number.

The driver continued down Little Lake Drive. George was still stunned by the image of the regal Charlotte looking like the homespun... what? hausfrau? The ex-resident agent of a phony charity. "Is anyone else going to run the CEA for Mr. and Mrs. Williams?"

"I heard someone say that other people in the Charity are gonna run it from Luanda. That's in Angola. They say it should be easier to manage right there in Africa. The mission supplies are supposed to be handled out of Luanda, too. But it is a relief to hear good things about some of those rebel countries."

"Who handled the supplies here in the Caymans?"

"I don't know. They weren't the type of charity that went around with their hat out asking people to put money in it. Mr. Williams would load his boat with supplies and they'd sail away for a few months. I actually don't know how the supplies got over there. If the supplies were handled locally, I guess they're out of business, same as the CEA. That's all I know."

George fished. "That's the domino effect. And I hear it all started with blood that wasn't properly screened. Mr. Williams got injured and they gave him a transfusion... bad blood. I heard that's what happened."

"Yep. Just goes to show ya. One little mistake. What's that theory people talk about? A butterfly starts a hurricane?"

"I think that's called the Chaos Theory. I'm not sure about that. But I get your point. One bad blood transfusion, and CEA has to shut down; and then their supply company has to shut down. I hope the dominos stop falling before they get to the people the missions helped. There's been enough 'chaos' from that one mistake."

The cab had pulled up to the curb in front of the Lamark Hotel. "Any place else I can take ya?" the cabbie asked.

"It might be interesting to get a few shots of the ship he used to deliver the supplies to the missions. Do you happen to know the name of Mr. Williams' ship?"

"No. But you could try the Maritime Registry Office."

"Sounds good to me. Let's go there."

At the office, appearing to be as friendly as possible, George asked, "I'm trying to locate a vessel owned by a fellow named Martin Williams. Do you have a ship registered by him?"

"I'd say 'Pleasure or commercial?' but I know the vessel. The *Sesame*. Beautiful ketch. It's in the Barcadere now."

"I'll go take a look at it in the marina now. I was supposed to write an article about the Williams' charitable works; but I just learned that they retired from missionary work because Mr. Williams got sick. Well... as long as I'm here, maybe I'll take a few shots of the Sesame and then book a sailboat ride."

"It's the best time of year to go sailin'," the clerk said.

"I saw the sunset last night," George agreed. "It was red and beautiful. And this morning the sky was bright and blue, no red at all."

"You got it! *Red sky in the mornin', sailor take warnin'. Red sky at night, sailor's delight.'* Words to live by." He smiled and George smiled back and gave him a quick salute.

Charlotte, dressed as Harriet Williams, stopped at the post office to pick up mail that had come to her via General Delivery. She smiled demurely at the postal clerk who asked how Mr. Williams was doing. "Fine," she said. "He's getting stronger every day. I have to rein him in. He wants to do too much, too soon. I'll tell him you were askin' for him."

She rode her three-wheeled bicycle down Little Lake Drive. It amused her to think that people assumed that using a bicycle for transportation distinguished her as a humble, frugal, and "good Christian lady who practiced what she preached." Harriet Williams did not put on airs and need to be driven everywhere. In fact, Charlotte knew of no better way to retain the firmness of her abdomen, thighs, and buttocks than to peddle herself around the island. She had a book that illustrated how to "keep in shape" doing housework; and, because she would not hire anyone to come into the house where her secrets might be uncovered, she did her own housework while she was "at home" in the Caymans. She also gave her forehead botox injections regularly and would not let a calendar day pass without doing one thousand "fish breathing" and "lion roaring" face-yoga exercises. She considered it a financial investment to purchase expensive cell generating face and neck creams. As Harriet Williams, she could not visit a spa or join a country club.

At her home on Little Lake Drive, she took the mail from the box at the driveway's entrance, looked through it and placed one envelope from Windhoek, Namibia in her purse as she walked to the front door. She entered the house, calling "Martin, Darling, I'm home."

"Did you get my prescription filled?" Martin gruffly called from the lanai.

"Of course." She placed the new pill bottles on the table.

Since he had developed AIDS, Martin's health had gone "up and down." Initially, he had responded well to the treatment he had received in Kingston. His prognosis was good and doubtless would have continued as such except that Charlotte happened to notice letters from Namibia in his bedside table when she went to pick him up and bring him home to Grand Cayman. She bribed a hospital orderly to let her photocopy the letters; and then she decided that his prognosis could never be allowed to be good again. The letters revealed that he was having a torrid affair with a boy in Namibia - a boy who was still in high school - and who seemed to have reason to believe Martin's promises that he would return to him and "share their lives" as they "lived like kings." Martin had evidently sent him considerable sums of money. This would have to stop.

Martin's health immediately went into decline as Charlotte sabotaged his anti-retroviral medicines. She had seen how Martin's attitude towards her son had altered, although, in one sense, she could hardly blame him. Henri had become such a simpering fool around Martin that it was impossible for anyone to show him proper respect. Martin, for example, had claimed that he contracted AIDS through a blood transfusion he had required because of an excessive nose bleed. Obviously, he had no bodily scars to account for a wound that required a transfusion; so he was forced to blame his nose. Everyone, except Henri, found this excuse laughable. And, no doubt, because Martin, too, regarded it as being so far-fetched that only an idiot would believe it, he began to humiliate her nobly born son, using him as he would use a common whore. Well, what could she do? She had no further need for Martin, but she did require whatever assets he owned - his interest in the house, his bank account, and his ownership of his ketch, the beautiful yacht, Sesame. She needed to have a long, business talk with Eric. Martin could not be allowed to draw up a new will or to transfer any more of his assets to an outsider.

"Did I get any mail?" Martin asked.

"No, just the usual bills. Ah, we've gotten a card from Henri. He says the roof contractor didn't show up as promised, but he's hopeful that he'll do the job before the end of the month. He sends his love and regards to you and insists that you rest." She looked at the picture of Mount Pelée in Martinique and then handed Martin the card. "What would you like for dinner? I passed Momma Lotte's restaurant on the way home from the post office. I could smell her creole shrimp."

"Yes, but have her put the shrimp over mashed yams, not rice. And pick up some tonic water and limes. Lots of limes. And buy a bottle of decent gin. Something with teeth in it."

"You're not supposed to drink alcohol."

"I didn't ask for a medical opinion. Just buy the gin."

"All right! Gin with teeth. I'll get two orders of the shrimp. But going to the grocery store for the tonic and limes will take a few more minutes. So be sure you take your 'before-eating' medicines on schedule."

Martin's AIDS anti-retroviral therapy required that he take four drugs, three times a day, plus one vitamin and mineral supplement. Two of the medications he took before meals, and two he took after eating. When he first returned from his cousin's house he could keep track of his medicines. But as Charlotte gradually replaced some of the pills with inert substances, he got noticeably weaker and tended to become confused. As his strength lessened, his irritability increased. She asked if he wanted anything else while she was out.

He said, "Pick me up a newspaper and a few magazines and don't take all day."

"All right," she called, heading for the door. "I'll be back as soon as I can. We can watch TV while we eat." Suddenly she stopped. "Listen," she said, almost as an afterthought, "I'm going to try to reach Eric to see if you can stay in his apartment while the real estate agent finally shows the place to clients this weekend. If I can't get through to Eric, I'll fix up the back room of the supply office. It won't kill you to spend a little time there. I'll make sure you get your medicines on schedule."

"You want me to stay in the Barracuda's back room? No! That is not acceptable!" Martin scowled. "If I can't stay in Eric's apartment, I won't stay in any windowless closet of a room. Have him pick me up in his VW and take me to the marina. I'll stay on Sesame."

"We'll just have to talk to Eric. If he has vacated his apartment but not yet turned in the keys, we can put some furniture in there for you. I don't know about utilities. If he's turned them off then we'll have to go to the supply company office. Henri ordered those utilities turned off on the 29th - so you'll still have water and electricity until then. As soon as the roof's finished in Martinique, he'll be back. You can discuss your living arrangements with him then. I'm too busy to deal with it now."

"I'll live on the Sesame!"

"Then you'll have to hire someone to take care of you until Henri returns. I have too much to do straightening things out around here. And living on the water in your condition will just invite a case of pneumonia! Stop arguing with me. It isn't good for you." She left the house wondering how it was possible to hate someone as much as she hated Martin Williams. She had to make Eric a deal.

Meanwhile, before she did anything else, she would have to go to the boys' phony supply company office and steam open the letter that had just arrived for Martin.

At the Barracuda Supply Company's barren office she went to the back room which consisted of a storage area and a bathroom. She wet a towel, turned on her hair dryer, and put the letter on the other side of the wet towel. The damp hot air loosened the glue in a couple of minutes. Using a fingernail, she teased the flap, and in another minute she had the envelope open. The letter was written in a childish hand and there obviously was an attempt to write in code.

Dear Mr. Williams,

The test sample I sent to the assay office came back and the result we hoped for was not to be had. The test was positive for pyrite. I am very sorry but I have faith that everything will turn out well. The assay officer says that we may need money to keep digging but that if we spend it wisely we can make the claim worth while. Your friends all miss you and wish you were here.

Your friend,
Punye.

"So," Charlotte said aloud, "he gave his new pet AIDS." She did not reseal the envelope, but put it in her purse and left the office to go to a printing shop to have it photocopied.

She peddled the bicycle past Eric's duplex and saw his VW parked outside. She could tell from the layer of dust on the windshield that he had not driven it in a week at least. She continued on and saw that his apartment windows were not shuttered. She did not call since Martin had gotten into the habit of looking through the phone bills and the less he knew of her business the better off she felt.

Besides, she was in her toothy, dowdy, drawn-on "bags under her eyes" Harriet Williams guise. To ask Eric a favor, she'd have to change into the second role she used in very brief visits to the Caymans. She would become Beatrix van Aken, an adventuress who leased the Piper from its owner, Charlotte La Fontaine. As a sexy, vibrant woman she would make Eric laugh and relax. It would be like old times. Eric always needed money and between having a good time with her in bed and having all that additional money, he would agree to help her.

She picked up the food and returned home. "Did you take your before-meal pills?"

"No," he said. "Did you get the tonic water and gin?"

"Yes, dear."

"Then I'll take them with a gin and tonic. Don't forget to put lots of lime juice on top."

As she squeezed the limes, she said cheerfully, "I'll keep the shrimp warm in the oven until your thirty minute wait is up. Meanwhile I'm going to take a shower and get ready to check at the hangar to be sure the Piper is perfectly tuned." She gave him his pills, put the shrimp in a warm oven, and went into her bedroom to prepare for a meeting with Eric.

Carrying a camera, George stopped at the Marina's office and asked the harbor master where he could find the ketch, Sesame.

"She's in port now," the master said. "Martin gonna sell it?" He walked outside with George and pointed out the ship.

"Not that I know of," George replied. "I was supposed to do an article on his charitable works in Africa. But he's not been feelin' well lately, so I'll get started on the article by taking a few pictures of the ship he used to carry supplies. Incidentally, do you know who delivered those supplies to him?"

"I think most of them came out of other countries. What he took on the Sesame he brought to the docks, himself."

"On another matter, do you get many Cuban vessels here?" George asked.

"Yes, more than you'd think." He turned and re-entered his office. "Holler if you need any help gettin' view angles."

George strolled along the pier, trying to look casual as he approached the Sesame. There might be a guard on board the vessel even though it was in the marina. "Ahoy, Sesame!" he called. No one came up from the cabin. Perhaps, George thought, someone guarded the ship only at night. If someone did, he might know more about the sailing associates of Harriet and Martin Williams. Also, if the suppliers sent goods to Christian missions, then the next place he would go would be to the Christian Supply Store. Surely they would know about their competition.

He found a phone directory and went to a shop that sold Bibles and books by a variety of Christian authors. The desk clerk was a young woman who did not even know who Martin or Harriet Williams was. Her mother, who owned the store, would be back behind the counter the following morning. George said he'd return. He asked himself if he should be surprised that even someone connected to a Christian supply store did not know who the eminent Christians in George Town were.

He stopped at an electronics store and looked over the surveillance camera set-ups they had. A camera that was on a 24 hour connection to a cellphone line that broadcast a video to a monitor was not the cheapest kind of recording apparatus available to him. Price was not, however, a consideration as far as George was concerned. "Can you get someone to install it on a public lamp post? The camera angle can be stationary." He gave the clerk the address he wanted surveilled.

"We probably can do it," the clerk said, "but you should be aware that the cost is not going to be as cheap as... shall we say, 'a legitimate' installation. Lamp posts are not supposed to be used for such purposes. We do have a very small camera that can get you a great picture and a great high def monitor you can set up in your hotel room and just sit back and watch the movie play. There's maintenance involved. The battery will last only so long."

"When can your man install it? The sooner, the better." He put his credit card on the counter. "I'm staying at the Lamark. Room 413."

The clerk took the card and went into the back room. George could hear him talking to someone. The clerk stepped back into the sales' room. "The address you're shooting is a house that's up for sale. You checkin' out potential buyers?"

"Yeah," George said, glomming onto a better excuse than the one he had. "It's a little salesmen's 'one-upmanship' - nothing more sinister than that."

"Ok. We'll get it up right away and deliver the monitor to you in your room. You gonna be there in the next couple hours?"

"Count on it!"

It was past lunch time. He walked back to the Lamark Hotel.

On the house phone he called Lily's room. No answer. He went into the restaurant and ordered lunch. By the time he finished he decided to contact Everett Smith. Maybe Sensei would be more forthcoming to

Lilyanne's father. If anyone could worm the information out of him, it was Everett.

He went to his room and placed the call.

As Charlotte left the house, she walked towards the avenue where she could get a cab to the airport. She looked back to see Martin standing at the window. She smiled, waved, and with her back to him again, she unbuttoned her shirt down to her bra line. As she turned the corner, her gait changed to a kind of frowsy walk. She did not take a cab. She tied her denim flying jacket around her waist and put her wide brimmed soft denim sun hat on with her big white rimmed sun glasses. She put a stick of chewing gum in her mouth and opened the flask of cologne she had brought with her and doused her breasts with it while she walked. She felt invincible with her hair down in flattering waves, her own perfect teeth showing in her smile, and wearing new makeup that made her look years younger.

Turning onto the street in which Eric's apartment was located, she strained to see if the shutters were still open. They were and she boldly went to his door and knocked.

Eric opened the door and stared at her. "Mom," he said, joking, and pulled her into the room as he shut and locked the door.

An hour later, as they lay in bed, he pronounced his opinion. "You know, you've gotten more body tone. You're firmer all over. I haven't seen you naked in months. What's your secret?"

"Being a slave to that bastard."

"All right. Out with it. What brings you here?"

"Eric, I can't continue to live with that monster. It's more than just having to look at him, although, God knows, the sight of his skin hanging on him like crescents in a Viennese drapery is enough to sicken anyone. It is how and why he betrayed us. Let me show you something." She got up and brought her tote bag to the bed. "Here are photocopies of letters he received while he was in the hospital in Kingston. They're all love letters from a boy. The last one of these says he feels sick and needs to get blood tests." She let Eric read it.

"The kid is scared. How old is he?"

"Fourteen or fifteen... he's a high school student! This came to the house today. It's code for a positive AIDS test. Martin actually gave this child - look at the handwriting! - AIDS. I don't care about myself. My concern is Henri. He's becoming more and more effeminate and accepting of the idea that he and Martin are going to live together as love partners in Martinique. If you read the letters you'll see that Martin intends to return to his Namibian boy. Henri doesn't even want to go back to France except to take Martin to a hospital in Paris. Or, for all I know, he thinks he'll come to his ancestral home and install Martin as the Master of the deLisle estate. Over my dead body! So that's my first objective. I must put an end to this romance."

"What's the second?"

"Martin didn't just happen to get diseased. You and I both know that he didn't get the disease from a bad blood transfusion for a bloody nose. His doctors in Kingston almost laughed in his face when he told them that. He laid with scum there in Angola or Namibia. I've seen his passport. He spent a lot of time in Namibia. He was supposed to be getting pictures taken with various politicians and rebel leaders for the Angola diamond-mine scam. Not one picture came out of this. He says he took them and they got lost. On top of non-performance he lies. He spent over two hundred thousand dollars on that trip. He says he bought expensive gifts for rebel leaders. Read these letters and you'll see who got the expensive gifts. Now to top it off he's actually in love with another boy! This will kill Henri."

"I could see that he cooled-off about Henri. But what's this got to do with me?"

"Martin has his own bank account. His name and mine are on the title to the house. He also owns Sesame. That ketch is worth at least $900K. It's in perfect condition."

"He could probably get a million for it."

"Look... in another week your lease on this apartment will be up and so will the lease on the office. We're getting ready to show the house and the real estate agent has told me that if we want to sell the property, we can't have an AIDS patient lounging around the living room. He looks so ugly, Eric. His skin hangs on him like he's wearing an oversized Greek tunic. Rolls and rolls of useless skin. I've got to get him out of the house. I was wondering if he could stay here for a week or so... while the real estate agent shows the house."

"No. Impossible. First, as you can see, I've been taking my furniture up to the Brac. Most of the chairs and cabinets are already up there. The living room furniture, too. I've got the bed, bed tables, and the kitchen set and I'm done. I don't want anybody with AIDS sleeping in my bed. Martin doesn't give a shit about rules. His morals have gone... maybe he associated with us for too long. But I don't want him using anything of mine."

"Then can you help me to fix up the back room of the office? I could put a cot in there and maybe hook up a TV. That's all he does now... order me around and watch television."

'Yes, I could do that. I'll buy a cot we can use."

"No, I've got the cot and the TV and the towels and things. Can you pick me up in your VW and take me to the office and help me to set things up?"

"I'll do that, but don't ask me to take him in my car. I don't want him in there, either."

"All right. I can call a cab to move him. There is a problem. He wants to live on the Sesame. But I've just had it thoroughly cleaned in case it was put up for sale. Are you sure you're not interested in owning his yacht? His bank account? If you help me to get rid of him before he gets a chance to write a new will and leave everything to his new boyfriend, we can make a deal. It'll be worth plenty to me to separate him from Henri."

Eric Haffner was not sufficiently gullible to believe Charlotte's tempting offer. And he wasn't going to help her to get rid of Martin and then have her disappear into France and leave him "holding the bag." He had to stall. Saying "No," outright would only invite trouble. "You'll have to talk to me about that again," he said. "I've ordered furniture made in Kingston and some artwork. We can talk about it when I get back. I've got to get the rest of my stuff out of here."

"When will you be back?"

"I should be back by the 27th. If you want to take charge of Martin's destiny, then this is what you should do. Go get yourself a bottle of *Everclear* or pure ethanol. I know that he's still drinking. That stuff's nearly 200 proof. Make a few appointments with key people... the real estate agent... somebody at the market... or at church... and just before he is supposed to meet the person, make him a drink. He likes lime so what you should do is put the alcohol at the bottom of the glass and then add ice and then the tonic water, and on top pour the lime juice. Because he also likes the taste of gin, put a little on the top of the lime so that it's the first thing that his tongue recognizes. Make sure you start the meeting before the alcohol has a chance to hit him. He'll start out seeming to be perfectly sober, but he'll start acting batty in ten or fifteen minutes. When you tell people that he's having severe emotional problems, they'll believe you. I've got some ethanol I can give you now to get the process started. Go home, call the agent, mix Martin a drink, and get the cot and the TV ready. I'll pick you up in half an hour and we can get the back room fixed up for him."

Leonardo did not understand what was going on. Ever since Lilyanne went out on deck, the captain was acting strangely. He spent hours sitting alone in the bow. He barely slept and ate. His eyes were bloodshot but he was not drinking. They were in Cuban waters and, by nightfall, they'd be docking in La Trinidad. He did not know what to expect. He spoke to Hugo and Hugo had no idea whatsoever what was going on. He did not dare speak to Lilyanne.

Martin Williams Shannon, known in the Caymans as Martin S. Williams, lay upon a deck chair watching a television soap opera he had gotten interested in while he was hospitalized in Kingston.

Charlotte, still wearing her Beatrix van Aken guise, brazenly walked into the Williams' house and went into the storage room to remove a cot; a pillow; a sheet, pillow case, and blanket; and carried them to the front lawn. She called to Martin. "Have you taken your after-dinner medicine, Darling?"

"No," he called. "I need more tonic water and lime... and put some gin in it!"

She called the agent and asked him to come to the house immediately. Then she brought her tote bag to the kitchen and opened the ethanol. She took a twelve ounce tumbler and made the drink exactly as Eric had directed. She quickly removed her makeup, changed her hair style and her clothes, drew a few dark lines around her eyes, and put her dental plate into her mouth in time to greet the real estate agent at the front door.

The agent was concerned. "What's up?" he asked.

"Martin is acting so strangely," she said. "Come back and talk to him."

She led the agent back to the patio, bringing with her the drink she had made for Martin. "May I fix you a gin and tonic?" she asked the agent.

"Yes," he said, turning to Martin and noticing what he was watching on TV. "I watch this, too," he said. "My wife got me hooked."

Martin laughed. "I started to watch it while I was in the hospital in Kingston. It does have a way to keep you coming back for the next episode."

They watched the screen and did not speak until the BBC soap opera had ended. By that time the alcohol had taken effect. Martin's demeanor completely changed. The friendliness was gone and in its place was contemptuous arrogance. "So you'll bring maybe ten people to my house," he said, slurring the words slightly as his head bobbed erratically, "and for that you think you're entitled to six percent of the price? Watta' joke! It's highway robbery. Why don't you stick a gun in my ribs. You're slick. That's what you are. Slick. A slick thief!"

Charlotte put her finger to her lips, indicating to the agent that he shouldn't respond. She led him from the patio into the house. "One minute he's the old Martin... so pleasant!" she whispered. "But the next minute... well, you've seen for yourself. I've truly got to get him out of the house before you bring potential buyers here."

"Definitely! I'm appalled. If he should suddenly talk to the prospectives... well, they'll all walk out."

Eric had arrived. He quickly loaded the cot into his car. "Where's the TV?" he asked.

"Back in one of the bedrooms; but try to avoid Martin. He's having one of his fits." Charlotte walked the agent to his car. "Mr. van Aken will provide a place for Martin to stay. I'll take my husband to his apartment. He'll be able to rest there while you show the house."

"Thank you, Harriet. I'm so glad you called me." He got in his car and left.

Everett Smith pleaded a reluctance to inject himself into the investigation. "I have such a poor track-record when it comes to meddling in Lily's affairs. If you think I should question Sensei Wong I will certainly do so. Just give me the word."

"You now have 'the word.' He's my best friend and business associate, and he wouldn't tell me squat. But he's got a lot of respect for you. He might not mind facing me with his religious shield in his hand, but he'd think twice about being confrontational with you. What I mean is, he knows how I feel about Lilyanne... but he also knows that your love is pure parental love... uncomplicated by romantic prejudices." George was surprised to hear himself admit that he had "romantic" feelings for Lilyanne. He had kept that information secret.

"I'll go immediately and call you back with whatever I learn."

Everett Smith visited Sensei without calling first for an appointment. He knew how the priest had reacted to George and did not want to give him an opportunity to decline to speak to him. At 4:30 p.m. his driver slowly drove down Germantown Avenue looking for a place to park. "Drop me off at the curb," Everett said. "Keep circling the block. I shouldn't be long."

"Sensei," Everett began, "I know you to be an honest and fair man. My only child's life is in danger. She has cried out for help; and I am sick with worry. She called on Sunday evening. We haven't heard a word from her since then. At the very least she would have called to let us know that her call was a false alarm. We've heard nothing. I'm begging you. If you know anything that could possibly be of help, please tell me. I know she went to the Caymans and I know which hotel she's registered in. But she hasn't been in her room since Saturday. I'm not asking you to tell me the nature of your discussion with her. But anything you can tell us about where she might be down there..."

Sensei weighed confidentiality against the need to help someone who could be in serious trouble. He decided to give a limited amount of information. "Last year, on a pier in the Barcadere Marina she thinks she saw Eric, the chauffeur. He was loading supplies on a ship called the Remittman. That's all I can tell you."

Everett Smith thanked him and went outside to call George.

George took the call and was so grateful for the information that Smith had to remind him that he, Smith, was the client and that passing on the information was the least he could do.

George wanted to go immediately to the Barcadere Marina, but he had to wait for the electronics' camera installer to show up with the monitor.

By 6 p.m. the man came and showed George how to operate the monitor. George gave him an extra large tip for his thoroughness. As soon as the man left, he went to the Barcadere Marina.

George wanted to keep a low profile as he prowled the docks and piers of the marina. He did not want to arouse the suspicions of the harbor master by inquiring about the location of the Remittman. His inquiries about the Sesame had raised enough interest.

There was a bar at the end of the marina, near the commercial wharf. He stopped in "for a pint" and nursed it through an hour's worth of listening to a dozen different conversations in foreign languages.

He asked the bartender if he knew of a sailing ship named the Remittman, but the bartender merely shrugged and advised, "Check with the Registry in the morning." George said he would and walked back to his hotel.

The message light was lit on his room phone. He pressed the button and heard Chief Inspector Bruce Alan-Royce's message: "We've just had an unidentified female delivered to the morgue. I didn't get a physical description of the girl you're looking for, but if you get this message before 8 p.m. call me and I can discuss physical descriptions with you to rule her in or out. Other than that the morgue opens at 9 a.m. and you can look at the body in the morning."

George looked at his watch. It was 9 p.m. The call had come in at 7:30. He did not think that he could last the night without knowing about the female in the morgue. He tried to call the Inspector but learned only that he had gone for the day. He tried to call the morgue, but calls from the public were not accepted after 8 p.m.

He tried to sleep. It was impossible. He got up and got dressed and walked to the address the phone book had given for the morgue.

The night attendant was sitting at a desk watching a monitor that played DVDs. As George pushed upon the entrance's swinging door, the attendant turned off the monitor. "Can I help you?" he said warily.

"The female they brought in earlier tonight, was she Chinese?"

"No. Caucasian."

"Hmm. How old would you guess she was?"

"I'm a lousy judge of age," he said, "especially when they're fat. She must have weighed 250 pounds. Forty... fifty. Collapsed while water skiing. Her sister identified her. She was even fatter."

"It's something to think about when you want to get off your diet."

He returned to the Lamark and stripped off his clothes, took a shower, studied the monitor's recordings, and fell into deep and grateful sleep.

WEDNESDAY, FEBRUARY 22, 2012

The Santiago's motor suddenly started. Lilyanne could feel the difference in the ship's movements. She must have dozed off, she thought. She listened intently to the sounds inside the cabin, but she could hear nothing. All three men were on deck.

She heard the ship being eased into its slip and Hugo jump down to tie the line to a cleat.

She heard the motor shut off. Her heart began to race and she braced herself to be dragged ashore by harbor police. "No," she told herself. "I have convictions. I'm going to slow my heart down and face them with my dignity intact. I cannot forget my mission. And today is Ash Wednesday." The date comforted her. It was a sign that a sacrifice of forty days... or of many forty days... had just begun. She laughed to herself about all the foolish things people gave up for Lent. "I'll be giving up my freedom and I'll consider myself lucky if that's all I have to give up."

For the next few minutes she did a deep breathing exercise and could literally feel her heart begin to slow down. Her hands had been clammy. She reached into her tote bag and took out a tube of hand cream and rubbed some of the fragrant cream into her hands. "I'm ready," she whispered.

Leonardo entered the cabin. "Shh!" he said. "Don't make any noise and get down under the blanket in case anyone should come in here. I'm supposed to stay in here and keep you quiet until the captain comes back."

"When will that be?" she whispered.

"It could be a couple of days. It could be in an hour. I don't know."

"Where did he go? What time is it now?"

"I don't know where he went. Hugo's on deck pretending to be fixing one of our running lights. It's just after midnight. We should have made landfall hours ago, but the old man lowered one of the sails and just stayed at the wheel thinking... thinking. Then he made up his mind about whatever he was thinking about. 'Raise the Genoa Jib,' he says. Then we started to move. I don't know what the hell is going on."

"I must have slept through all of that. I didn't hear anything."

"He put one of his tranquilizer pills in your soda can. I think he didn't want you to interfere with whatever he was deciding to do."

"Well... he succeeded. What do we do now?"

"Wait quietly. You cannot go up on deck. If you have to pee, I'm supposed to give you those plastic cups you gave me when we started. I never was able to take the trash anywhere so he told me to fish one out and make sure it didn't leak."

"That was thoughtful," she said, grinning. "Right now, I'd like to use one... if you don't mind."

"Ok," Leonardo said. "But I can't leave the cabin and you can't leave the bunk."

Lilyanne sighed. It all came under the heading of "conviction."

It was after 9 a.m. when George entered the Maritime Authority Offices to ask for the owner's name of the Remittman. He spoke to the same clerk he had spoken to the day before.

"How was your sailing excursion?" the clerk asked.

For a moment George did not know what he was talking about. He suddenly remembered and said, "Ah, I didn't go. I got a call from my boss and it disrupted my whole day."

"I know how *that* is," the clerk said, looking over his shoulder. "You want Claus van Aken. He keeps the Remittman at the Barcadere."

"Thanks, Captain," George tried to sound friendly. "Do you have a home address for van Aken?"

"Second floor, 2201 Carruthers," he read from a computer screen.

"Again... my thanks. I owe ya' one!"

Outside he hailed a cab and asked to be taken to the address. He could see the front door standing open as he went up the stairs. A cleaning lady was running a vacuum cleaner. George stood in the doorway and startled her. She shut off the vacuum. "You here to rent the place?"

"No, I'm looking for Claus van Aken."

"His lease was up and he left. Gave the owner extra time to find a new tenant."

"Do you know where Mr. van Aken moved to?"

"Somebody said something about him buyin' a place on Cayman Brac. Can't tell you any more than that." She turned on the vacuum and continued to stroke the rug.

"I was here yesterday," George said to the man occupying the master's chair at the Marina. "My editor wants me to check out another ship... Claus van Aken's *Remittman*. Can you tell me where she's berthed?"

"I can tell you where she *was* berthed, but since she's gone I can't tell you where she *is* berthed or if she's berthed at all. Claus left for Kingston, Jamaica, yesterday."

"Any idea when she'll be back here?"

"He was light on crew so I give him three days to get there and three to get back, plus whatever time Claus spends in Kingston. I'll start lookin' for him to be here in a week."

"Thanks," George said, feeling his legs go numb and his brain begin to ossify as he contemplated hanging around doing nothing for a week. He walked stiffly back to his hotel, knocked fruitlessly on Lilyanne's door, let himself into his own room, flopped on the bed, and groaned. It was a disappointment for which he was not prepared.

As he lay on his bed it occurred to him that Lilyanne did not have to be on the Remittman. Maybe this was a good sign. If Eric had business in Kingston, he wouldn't have taken Lilyanne with him. George did not know that Eric Haffner had no intention of going to Kingston. Eric was simply not in the mood to help Charlotte dispose of Martin or do to him whatever her devious mind had planned to do.

George called room service and asked for a pot of coffee and some pastries. Then he called Beryl.

"I could use a woman's angle," he said. "All I know is that on Sunday evening she called me on a Cuban phone and that she's registered in this hotel and hasn't been in her room - as far as the hotel people know - since Saturday. All I can surmise is that if she has blundered into Cuban territory she is at least in safe hands if the authorities have her. I'd like you to ask Smith to contact one of his friends in the State Department and get directed to one of the agencies who handle Cuban affairs. It may take a month for them to get around to notifying anybody, but at least she'll be safe.

"I've ordered a high-priced surveillance set up on the Williams' house. The monitor is here in my room. Nothing much is goin' on there. I've seen Charlotte looking like two different women, none of them Charlotte. The house is up for sale and for that reason alone I don't see them holding Lily prisoner in it. But they're all we've got at the moment. Eric Haffner is using the name Claus van Aken and he's on his way now to Jamaica. When the opportunity comes up, I'll enter the Williams' house and check it thoroughly to see whether there's any evidence of Lily's being there... or where they might be heading next."

"It would help," Beryl noted, "if we had some idea why Lilyanne went down there. It doesn't make a lot of sense. She was obviously troubled by something, or else she wouldn't have called Sensei. Everett says she was brooding and lost weight. I'm hoping she didn't intend to confront them."

"That's the problem. She's here because they're here. There is absolutely no other reason for her to be here but that she's conducting some kind of investigation or vendetta. Beryl, this scares the hell out of me. She is no match for one of them, let alone all four."

"So, Eric's flown the coop to Jamaica? Is it possible that he got wind of a detective's being on his trail?"

"No. I don't see how... unless he saw me and I didn't see him. I got in late Monday evening. It's Wednesday afternoon. From what the cleaning lady said, he had left early so that they'd have more time to show the place. He must have intended to leave by the end of the month. This coincides with the sale of the Williams' house. They must be winding-down their Cayman activities. Yet, the harbor master expected Eric back. I don't know where the others intend to go, but he's got his personal space rented at the marina and nobody seems to think he's going to give it up."

"You haven't seen Henri. He could be wherever Eric is."

"I doubt that. Eric plans to continue to live here. The cleaning gal heard that he bought a place on Cayman Brac. But the others are heading out. Why else would they be selling the house? If you recall, Henri told Lilyanne that they had another home on Martinique. It was up on the Northwest coast and had once been buried beneath a thick blanket of pumice when Mount Pelée erupted. It was restored years ago. But it *was* La Fontaine property. Cecelia Smith went to the Sorbonne and knows a zillion French bureaucrats or whatever they're called. What I'd also like you to do is to ask her to use her contacts to surreptitiously inquire about the occupancy of their home in the northwest of the Island."

"That's a good idea. A very good idea. I'll get right on it."

"She can also make an inquiry about that Three Cedars estate they have in the Alpine foothills."

"Good idea. Henri could be there."

"If Eric has moved to another island then there's no point in our worrying about the supply company. They probably closed it down the same time that they closed down the CEA. As long as you're putting Cecelia to work, ask her to check the property records for the name 'van Aken.' I'm going to check them here, but she can also find out if the van Aken name turns up in Martinique. There are probably a zillion van Akens in Europe so tell her not to squander her resources on checking there."

"I personally don't like the coincidence of Lilyanne going to the Caymans at this critical point when the four swindlers are apparently dispersing. Time is not on our side. I'll get busy and keep in touch."

Cecelia Smith was enthusiastic about helping. "I checked them out two years ago. They did at that time own places in Martinique - I have it written down upstairs - and in the Rhone-Alps area. I even have photographs of both houses. I will call Paris in the morning - it is simply too late to call now. But trust me on this. I will find out who, if anyone, is living in those two houses."

Beryl thanked her and called George who had just returned from the tax recorder's office. There was no property owned by Claus van Aken.

Day faded into night aboard the Santiago. Hugo wanted to go ashore to purchase some food for them, but, considering the kind of trouble he'd face if he disobeyed an order, he instead tried to liven the task of eating combat ration packs from Russia. "We can be glad it does not say CCCP on the box." They managed to be quietly light-hearted sitting in the dark with only a tiny flashlight.

There had been no word from Captain Quintero; and, following his instructions, they could do nothing but wait.

THURSDAY, FEBRUARY 23, 2012

Paris, being six hours ahead of Philadelphia, received calls from Cecelia Smith starting at 4 a.m. her time. She "called in a few markers" and had several old friends pull the necessary strings to get discreet law enforcement people to check on the inhabitants in Les Trois Cedres of eastern France and in Les Falaises, the La Fontaine home in northwest Martinique.

George, while studying the little monitor, ordered room service for breakfast. Cecelia's call came into his iPhone. "Madame, La Contesse, ain't at home," she said jokingly, "and neither is the rest of the royal family. A servant did say that she was expected - but not "Monsieur, Le Conte' - within a month or so. Charlotte must still be on her knees planting pansies in her front yard."

"Then we can cross off France... but not Martinique."

"I'll call you back when I hear about their Island residence." Cecelia disconnected the call. George grinned. It was good to have her as an ally.

As the sun came up high enough to illuminate both sides of the street, the camera picked up Harriet Williams once again tidying the front yard, preparing it for the real estate walk-through the next day.

A few hours later George received Cecelia's second report. "Henri La Fontaine was definitely in residence in Martinique. The observer noticed servants of some kind around the house. There was a roof installation ongoing. He had flown over the property and wasn't in a position to see anyone specifically. He took some aerial shots. The property looks the same as it did when I saw photographs of it a couple of years ago. It was by inquiring at the local post office that he learned that Henri was actually there." Cecelia had spoken rapidly and was out of breath. "Anything else?" she asked.

"Not at the moment," George replied, googling a map of the Caribbean. "I see it's 1400 miles to Martinique. If I don't get any other leads, maybe it would pay me to go there."

"Yes," agreed Cecelia. "Play it as it lays."

For George, where Lilyanne Smith was concerned, there was no such thing as "playing it as it lays."

It was mid-morning when Captain Quintero returned to the Santiago, carrying a shopping bag of fresh fruit, bread, and cheese. He seemed to be a different man. His movements were more graceful and his voice was not so sharp.

"Cast off," he said simply, and Hugo jumped down onto the pier to untie the line and toss it up to Leonardo.

In ten minutes they were out of the harbor and Quintero ordered the sails to be raised. Lilyanne could feel and hear the sails' luff and then the captain would tack to one side and then to another. She did not know where they were going, but from the shifts in direction that she could sense the boat making, she wondered how long it would take them to get anywhere.

Finally, the captain called her on deck. "I'm taking you back to the Caymans. I called the Marina. I have friends there. The man you're looking for - the one who owns Remittman, has a place in Cayman Brac. His name is Claus van Aken. I'm not going to try to influence you in your decision. If you want to go back to George Town, I'll take you there. If you want to go to Cayman Brac, I'll take you there. Which is it? You have time to think it over."

"Cayman Brac."

"May God be with you."

"Thank you. Did you see Francisco?"

"Yes. He forgave me. I cried, so he pretty much had to. I slept well last night. My wife said I slept ten hours. Thank you for your new ethics.

You'll have to write a book about it and mail me a copy. Now go below. The sea is getting difficult."

"I worry that you will have to pay your men extra. May I compensate you for that?"

"No. Hugo owes me a favor, and Leonardo is lucky he is not in jail along side a pretty stowaway. Go below now."

George studied the monitor. A cab pulled up to the house. The cabbie went to the door and rang the bell. Charlotte came out of the house and walked beside Martin. This man was a caricature of the man in the blackmail photos. He walked with a cane. His clothing was loose. He shuffled rather than stepped. "Frankly," George said to himself, "he looks plastered." Charlotte opened the mailbox and put the group of letters in her purse. The cabbie opened the car door and Martin got in. Charlotte went to the opposite door and got in. The cab drove away.

George immediately left the hotel, hailed a cab, and went to the Williams' house.

He did not hesitate. Asking the cabbie to wait, he hurried to the front door and both knocked and rang the bell. He looked in a window and seeing no activity, he walked around to the rear of the house, stopping on the way to look inside each window for any sign that Lilyanne was there. In the lanai, he tried the kitchen door. It was locked. He took out a folder of lock picks and opened the door. He went from room to room calling Lilyanne, checking to see that there was no attic or basement that he had possibly overlooked. There was absolutely no indication that Lilyanne was there or had ever been there. He exited the house via the back door and making sure the door was locked, he went to the cab and returned to his hotel.

He called Everett and gave him a detailed account of all that he had done to track Lilyanne down.

Everett had a theory. "If Henri is on Martinique, fixing the place up, he's probably getting it ready to live in. After all, he's not expected back in France. Charlotte is. Eric is evidently sailing alone - if that's what the harbor master meant by being 'light on crew' - and the fourth one has

AIDS. I'm thinking that maybe Henri does plan to have Lilyanne with him. He might have used some Cuban friends to take her off Grand Cayman and deliver her to Martinique. I'm not saying that he necessarily plans a kidnapped bride scenario, it could just be that she was ready to tell the authorities about the CEA and the source of his income." Everett's voice softened. He remembered the night in Cape May when he and Henri sang, *I'm the man who broke the bank at Monte Carlo.* "You know, much of that trouble really didn't involve Henri. He wasn't in the photos and he was constantly having to live under the regime of that harridan Charlotte. Maybe he really did love Lily... and we know Lily did love him."

George was speechless. He did not know what to say. He would have been justified in telling Everett Smith that he was a jackass of the worst sort, a gullible fool, an idiot, and so on. George thought of many names that would fit the occasion of painting Henri in an angelic pose. He said nothing as Smith continued.

"If she were on a sailing ship, it would take ten days or two weeks, on average, to sail from the Caymans to Martinique. Motorized, even less. She could be on her way there now. If they're delivering her to him, I doubt that they'd lay a hand on her. I'm expressing a hope, I know. It's possible that Henri is waiting to receive her in Martinique. It might not be a bad idea to look for her there."

George did not know how to comment on the possibility of a romantic tie between Lily and Henri. He had already thought about going to Martinique. He decided to remain cooperative and professional. "Fourteen hundred miles is not a very long distance by plane. So you're thinking I should take a side trip to Martinique? With Eric gone and Charlotte tending a sick man and selling their home here... Martinique is all we've got. If Lily's here on this island, I've looked everywhere I know to look."

"Then, yes, take a trip to Martinique. Rent a car and drive up to his house. See for yourself if she's there. Make him tell you what he has planned for my daughter. It is no coincidence that she was at the Caymans. She was looking for them... or I should say, for him."

George was still trying to control his anger when the call mercifully ended. He called Beryl to get her input. He stated all the things he could not believe that he had heard. She interrupted him. "George, he's her father. To a father, every man in the world wants his daughter. So forget that sweet guy Henri La Fontaine. If he's got her, it may be exactly what Everett first said... he wanted to prevent her from ratting him out. As far as Martinique is concerned, I have to agree with Everett. There is activity at Henri's isolated home. Nothin's happening anywhere else. Check it out. You've got time to kill until Eric returns from Kingston."

George made reservations on the next flight to Le Lamentin, Martinique. He would leave the next morning.

Later in the afternoon, the eastern sky grew dark, the winds shifted, the jib filled and Santiago began to run with the wind.

FRIDAY, FEBRUARY 24, 2012

All night Santiago continued to skim the water. By morning, in less time than Lilyanne had supposed it would take, the ship approached Cayman Brac, the closest of the Cayman Islands to Cuba.

"Look!" Captain Quintero called to Lilyanne, "There is your lighthouse. Cayman Brac is right off our port side."

Lilyanne rushed to the side of the ship and saw in the distance ahead the sun glinting off the old metal lighthouses of the "Brac" or bluff. "It looks like a pirate's hideout."

"If I'm not mistaken," Quintero said, "it once was. I've been there a few times. I hope you find your friend or enemy there. If not, maybe you can spend a few weeks to get some good food in you and some sun on you. You've been inside and hungry long enough."

"I can't argue about that," Lilyanne said, concealing her eagerness to get ashore.

The harbor master in George Town had given Captain Quintero GPS coordinates for the harbor nearest Eric's property, yet when the Santiago entered the designated harbor, the white hulled sloop was not anchored there. There was no formal marina anywhere on the island; and ships had to find shelter wherever they could. At this little harbor, a dozen vessels appeared to be moored in little clusters around a buoy or individually anchored. Since the harbor was merely a small bay in the coastline, it revealed all of its nautical guests at a glance. The Remittman was not there.

Lilyanne was on deck studying the vessels. The captain spoke gently to her. "There's a hotel on shore. He may have gone to buy something at the end of the island, or he may not be on the island at all. If you want to be taken ashore, Hugo will take you in the dinghy."

"Yes, I'd like to go ashore," she said.

He ordered Hugo to bring the dinghy alongside. Then he took Lilyanne's hand and helped her to climb down the boarding ladder. "I'm going to buy a newspaper every time I'm in George Town. Don't let me read your obituary there. When you are safely at home, call the Barcadere Marina and leave a message for me."

"I will," she said. "*Gracias*."

"*Vaya con Dios*," he said, and quickly turned away.

Lilyanne Smith stepped out of the dinghy onto land that seemed to sway beneath her feet. She kept trying to balance herself on an earthen platform that was solid and stable. She turned and waved goodbye to Hugo and Leonardo who stood on the ship watching. The captain was nowhere in sight.

She soon found herself looking in the mirror of the ladies' room of the hotel restaurant. She looked homeless, half-starved and dirty. There was a shop in the hotel that sold casual garments, sun screen lotion, boat maintenance items, and rudimentary fishing tackle. She decided to check in for the night, but hesitated, wondering if she had enough cash to pay for at least one night there. She inquired about room rates and discovered that she had enough cash to pay for an entire week; but she did not think she'd be spending a week. "No," she whispered aloud to herself, echoing MacBeth, "If it were done when 'tis done, then 'twere well it were done quickly." She did not see any daggers hanging before her so she stopped at the fishing tackle end of the shop and bought a knife suitable for gutting fish.

"Do you happen to know Claus van Aken?" she asked the desk clerk.

"Sure. He comes here every day. His place is at the top of that road outside. It says 'Porter's Mining' but he never changed the name after he bought and renovated it. He's up there now. If you want to walk up to his house, you need to put better shoes on. The road's not paved and the stones are loose and sharp. You'll slip and slide on them and they'll cut your feet. There are crevices alongside that road. You don't want to fall off the side. We sell sneakers."

Lilyanne bought a pair of shoes and also new underwear, blouse, skirt, and an extra pair of sandals. She checked into the hotel, ate an enormous dinner, and argued with herself about calling her father while she took a deluging shower. In the world outside her room, a spring storm pounded the island.

She thought about George and wanted to call him; but there was her "mission" to consider. She needed to examine the possibilities, and if she called George, he would trace the call back to Cayman Brac. Credit cards... phones... She had to avoid such complications. As it was, it was still possible that George had traced that call back to Cuba or to the shipping lanes between Cuba and the Caymans. He wouldn't know where to begin to look for her. But if he found out, he would come to Cayman Brac to try to stop her from doing whatever she had decided to do about Eric.

She had eaten too much and was too tired. She could not think about forgiveness or punishment or making ethical decisions. Right now, she wanted to sleep in a bed that didn't move. In the morning her sea legs would be a thing of the past. She would eat more and sleep more and then make up her mind. She found it comforting to listen to the rolling thunder. In five minutes she was beyond hearing anything at all.

For the benefit of the cab driver, Charlotte tried to sound maternal in her "Harriet" voice. "Martin, Darling," she coaxed, "the real estate walk through might be over sooner than we think. If it is, I'll come and get you." She held up a paper bag. "Meanwhile, your pills are all here. The TV is working. You've got everything you need in there... tissues... toilet paper... and even limes and tonic water in the little refrigerator."

As the cab stopped, Martin grunted. "There ain't nobody looking at the house! You got somebody else comin' to the house tonight? Well, I'm not sleepin' here. Get this through your head," he snarled. "I am not spending the night alone in a closet. If you don't come and get me, I'll go to the Sesame myself."

"Martin... please don't be difficult," she whined. "I'm doing my best." As she removed her change purse to pay the cabbie, she also removed mail. Martin immediately saw the letter from Namibia on top. "I guess we can wait to go over the bills," she said, groping for change.

He reached for the foreign airmail-striped envelope. "Give me that one," he ordered.

"All right, dear." She gave him the boy's letter. Then she turned to the cabbie. "Maybe you should wait. He doesn't like company when he gets like this." The cabbie nodded.

Martin stumbled out of the cab. "Don't you have to get back to the house? Then go! Just come back for me later."

Charlotte affected a wounded look and pretended to be helping him to enter the Office. When he got into the back room, she turned back to the street and gave the cab driver the address to her home. Immediately she began to daydream of ways she would kill the man in the back room of the supply company's office.

The real estate agent had shown the house to three couples and two single men who wanted privacy.

Charlotte smiled and told everyone that if she were needed, she would be out front, tending her garden. The women came out to ask her about the utility bills. She returned to the house and opened a desk drawer to show the ladies the actual bills. Not knowing that for many months of the year, nobody lived in the house and that the charges they saw were simply minimum service charges, they were all delighted to see how inexpensive the utilities were.

She gave each of them a map of the George Town area: the nearby schools, athletic field, public and private tennis courts and swim clubs. "We even have a wonderful dressage team here on the island if your children like to ride. You'll truly love living here."

"Where will you be going?" one lady asked.

Charlotte was momentarily stumped. She quickly invented a sister who lived in Atlanta and said she'd be visiting her and then would decide where to take up residence. She might, she allowed, start another mission... perhaps in Belize.

The real estate agent made appointments to speak with the prospective buyers at his office or on the phone. He turned to Charlotte. "I'll see you in the morning," he said cheerily. Everyone's attitude was so positive that she was certain that the agent would conclude the sale shortly. The main thing was getting the money and then getting rid of Martin. She called a cab and asked to be taken to the Barracuda Supply Company. She would have to offer to spend another night in Martin's company.

As the cab pulled up to the curb, she searched the empty office for a sliver of light under the door to the back room. There was no light. "Wait here a moment," she said to the driver. She entered the office and went to the back room. It was empty. She locked the office and told the cab driver to take her to the Barcadere.

From the place near the entrance at which the cab stopped, she could see that Sesame's lights were on. She paid the driver and went back to the yacht. "Ahoy Sesame!" she called.

Tommy, the night guard, came on deck and lowered the boarding ladder for her. She feigned concern. "Is Captain Williams all right?"

"Yes, Ma'am. He's fine. Just come to spend the night."

"Does he have enough to eat... and his medicines?"

"Yes, Ma'am. He's fine."

Charlotte went into the Captain's quarters. Martin was propped up on the bed watching TV. "Do you have everything you need?" she asked with a salesman's solicitude.

"Yes. Except peace and quiet. I don't feel like talkin."

"Would you like me to go home and let you rest here alone? I'd have to get a cab."

"You shouldn't have let the last one go until you checked with me. Go!"

"All right. If you'll rest easier with some time alone, I'll go out on the wharf and get a cab. Tommy will help me off the ship. What time do you want me to come tomorrow? You absolutely have to take your medicine on time."

"I will," he said dismissively. "Don't worry about me."

Charlotte left the ship and went home. She stretched out on her bedroom floor and did one hundred full pushups. The bicycle toned her lower body, but only pushups, she found, would keep the muscles of her upper arms and torso from getting flabby. She took an extra long hot shower before doing her maintenance and repair work. With a tiny brush she put eyelash lengthening liquid on her eyelids and rubbed her cell-stimulation cream into the skin of her face, neck, arms and hands. She sat before her mirror and did her facial yoga and cheek, neck, and jowl muscle-strengthening isometric exercises. Then she got into bed naked, pulled the sheet up to her neck, did ten cycles of a deep breathing kriya, and fell asleep, lulled by the images of seeing Martin lying in a coffin.

George deplaned, rented a car, consulted a map, and drove north to Saint Pierre and then left the highway to take the road up to Les Falaises. He looked at the house, situated on the cliff. It seemed so warm and inviting in its provincial style. Yes, he thought, it was "picture post card alluring." From a distance he could recognize hollyhocks standing sentinel before the walls; and as he got closer to the building he could see - though he could not name - larkspur, zinnias, asters and, finally, as he parked, portulaca. He supposed that the altitude permitted more northern flowers to grow there. He wondered for a moment if Lily - whether she had been abducted or not - might like to live there. She would enjoy the flowers and the isolation, the view of the sea. Maybe there was a piano inside. She had told him that she took music lessons for years, but he had never heard her play. He imagined her sitting at the piano playing Chopin. She would walk around the house and grounds wearing a long skirt.

A servant came out and addressed him in French. George did not understand him and kept repeating, "Henri La Fontaine? La maison de Henri La Fontaine?"

The servant launched a long apparently apologetic speech that so confounded George that he pushed the man aside and walked into the house. The cook who was working in the kitchen dried her hands and said, "His Lordship left yesterday. Nobody's home."

"When are you expecting him again?"

"He went to pick up his friend. They should be back within the month."

"Martin Williams?"

"Yes. Mr. Williams will be staying here, recuperating from an illness."

"Then they don't plan to stay long?"

"No, I think they'll be here for quite a while. We've been getting the house ready... the pantry's stocked."

"Has any young lady been here to visit, or are you expecting one to come by?"

The cook laughed. "Not at *this* house."

George smiled and shook his head, acknowledging the remark's intention. Then he thanked her, got into his car, and drove back to Le Lamentin.

Eric Haffner would have been thrilled to know that Lilyanne Smith was 120 feet below him. He had always admired her and, in fact, had a little crush on her. He had not thought that she was particularly attractive when he first encountered her, but when he saw her dressed and made up - especially on the night of the opera - so beautiful in velvet and jewels - he envied Henri and actually resented him for destroying something that he, Eric, wanted for himself. He liked her naiveté because it wasn't predicated on unintended ignorance of the world but rather on intended rejection of the world, a world for which he had nothing but contempt.

For more than a year he had worked on the eleven room office and residence mining property. It had not been a labor of love - one of those hobbies that are ends in themselves. No, his labor had a purpose, a practical purpose. When he cut himself or overworked his muscles, he griped as any workman would do. He was, he decided, free from the need to posture, to keep "the stiff upper lip" and bear his discomforts in the name of some egoistic game. This was honest, noble labor. Pain and suffering experienced while performing such feats as mountain climbing and in the mastery of sports were not noble. They were compensating exercises in self-denial by people who craved money and fame.

He had no construction experience and no tradesman's skills when it came to renovating the building he had purchased. Aside from his ability to follow instructions, he brought nothing to the task. He had always earned money by tricking people and this ability was of little use to him in replacing the clay roof tiles that had been smashed by a tree branch during 2004's *Hurricane Ivan*. He had removed partitions between four of the six of the small bedrooms that had once been used by mineworkers. He now had a guest bedroom, a nursery, a nanny's room, and a child's room. The other five rooms were left intact: kitchen; master bedroom; office - which would be his living room; map and blue print reading room - which would be his dining room; and the waiting room - which would be his foyer.

He often thought about the people he had tricked. Ninety-nine percent of them were fakes: peasants with large bank accounts who needed lessons in humility. They saw him in his chauffeur's uniform and imagined themselves to be his social superiors. His own family, on the other hand, was truly rich and superior and had been so for many generations. Rarely did he and his three "associates" get the opportunity to swindle "old money." Eric derived a special satisfaction from these conquests. He readily understood that there was an element of surrogation in this pleasure. He realized that he took pride in the very family who cursed and rejected him.

Especially around the holidays he missed his home in Vienna. At fifteen, he had been sent away to school in France because of his bad and somewhat licentious behavior; but in the twenty years since then that he had been away from home, many of his old adversaries had died. He was now almost as old as his father had been the last time he saw him. Yet he had no son to threaten or punish or, as might have been the case, to praise. For the holidays, then, he began to miss not having a family of his own. When he labored under the sun, repairing the roof or mixing concrete for the patio that he had added onto the office-residence, he thought of family picnics and of cooking outdoors. He built an outdoor patio and barbecue "to continue a tradition." He wanted to show that he was resourceful, that he could build something with his own hands that would show that he was "a man for all seasons." He looked disdainfully at men who dealt in banking and commerce and lived off the sweat and ideas of others. Even lower in his estimation were men who worked to become famous: athletes and novelists and corporate moguls and communist dictators. They were all the same.

Often, when he would lie in bed after a hard day of work, he would think about the woman with whom he wanted to share his life and home. Naturally, she wouldn't automatically love him. The marriage would be more in line with an aristocratic uniting of two great houses. She would admire his ancestral line and consider it a privilege to give him descendants created from both their houses.

Throughout the year of his "construction" ordeal, he often went to the bars and clubs in which there were women of the desired child-bearing age group to seek a suitable wife. He found none. Either they did not want to reside in his home on the bluff, or they were newly rich. He refused to lower his standards. He was a gentleman of taste and refinement. He spoke many languages and was well-read on many subjects. Somewhere there would have to be a woman who was rich, but not newly rich, and of genteel qualities so that he could keep her on his arm and go back to his home in Vienna with a blonde child or two, and say, "Look at what you missed out on." Or, possibly, "You thought you had destroyed me and that I could never manage without you. But I and my beautiful family are happy, while you are as miserable as you have always been."

The next time he was in George Town, he would buy a swing set for the back yard.

SATURDAY, FEBRUARY 25, 2012

Lilyanne was seated at a table even before breakfast was being served. She saw the kitchen help come into the hotel and listened to them start the coffee machine and the deep fryer for potatoes and start the grill for bacon and sausages. She had selected a seat by the window, and sitting there looking out on the gloom of a drizzly, foggy morning, she could see only a few people who had spent the night on their boat get up and head for the hotel's restaurant.

When the waitress approached, Lilyanne asked, "They have such expensive boats. Why don't they sleep on shore and get some decent rest?"

"Because of theft. You'd be surprised at the scum who steal boats. Honestly! They'd leave people marooned on a deserted island and make off with their boat. There's nothing worse than a thief. Sometimes the boat runs out of gas and they just abandon it. The Caribbean is filled with little countries that have accommodating laws about registration. Like anything else, crime seems to find a way."

"Do they steal sailboats, too?"

"Sure. If they know how to sail."

Lilyanne thanked her for the information and ordered breakfast which she took her time eating. Then she went to her room to think about her decision.

So Eric was now known by another name and, evidently, he had another mode of living. From the way the clerk in the hotel spoke about him, he was well-regarded. Certainly no one considered him a rapist, a thief, and a blackmailer. Did this mean that he had been saved by the grace of God? The clerk saw him every day. He had renovated a mining property... Porter's Mining. And this must be his residence. Surely, Charlotte and Henri did not live up there in a miner's building. But at the moment, they were not her concern. She was limiting her judgment to Eric Haffner. He was the one she came to confront and to determine whether he had obtained divine pardon and was living honorably or whether he was still intent on living dishonorably by victimizing others.

She began to doubt her ability and her right to judge Eric. She wished now that she had waited to complete Sensei's course instead of impulsively running down to the Caymans to confront Eric. "I'm not ready for the task," she told herself. "I've got to stop vacillating and recall my own distress. I wasn't ready to be a victim, either. Neither was Margaret." She began to remember Margaret's "confession" and the expression of regret on her face. "That will be the regret I feel if I don't stop him," she said aloud. "And that will be in addition to the nightmares and panic attacks and insomnia... and loss of appetite. I've become a wreck of a human being because I've been unable to act decisively. Well," she pep-talked herself, "I probably shouldn't have come, but I'm here now and whether or not I'm prepared to render a judgment and to act if I believe that he is still a monster, I've got to try to fulfill my mission."

Obviously, since she did manage to find herself on Cayman Brac, she did intend to come face to face with Eric Haffner. That settled it. Rain or no rain, she would not put the day of judgment off.

She put on her new walking shoes, brushed her teeth, and started out to confront Eric in his home.

The climb was steep and, because of so many loose sharp rocks, extremely slick. Not even the tennis-shoe tread on her sneakers provided any traction. Several times she slipped and only her long skirt prevented her knees from being skinned and bruised.

The sign had indicated that Porter's Mining had an altitude of 120 feet, and she reminded herself that this was the height of a twelve storey building. The path was not, however, an ascent on a clean, flat set of stair steps. Because of the switchbacks, the road was many times longer than 120 feet, and she had to walk slowly and cautiously and to stop and rest frequently. She had negotiated only two of the switchbacks when her shoes began to blister her feet and her long skirt became so wet from the downpour that it clung to her legs and actually inhibited her from walking. When she placed one leg forward, she had to pull the clinging skirt off her other leg. She wished she could just pick up her skirt, but not only would that be indecent but she'd also lose the protection the cloth afforded her.

She had no watch on and could only estimate that it was around 9 or 10 a.m. when she arrived at the summit. Exhausted and thirsty - despite the rain that dripped into her mouth - she had reached the limit of her endurance. She saw his house and looked to see if there were a porch or some overhanging feature that she could step under and get out of the rain and sit down. But there was no porch.

She did not see anyone, but she could hear the rhythmic sound of what seemed to be a hammer striking rock. She stopped to listen to the sound, trying to decide what it was and where it was coming from.

The house was strangely pretty, she thought. It was a square box in design, but Eric had painted it using the same visual trickery that she had seen in Japanese gardens. The façade was straight-line flat, with the entrance positioned in the middle, but four vertical lines had divided the front into five sections: the entrance and two sections on either side of it. He had painted the outermost sections light beige and the two inner sections darker tan. Decorative dark wood, including roof- supporting poles in the manner of Indian pueblos, created an interesting entryway. The overall effect was to make the lighter sections retreat and the darker sections come forward.

The windows and shutters, completing the suggestion of a southwest adobe style, were painted an antique bluish green that varied in tone according to the terms of the illusion.

It was cleverly done, she thought as she walked to the front windows and looked inside. The rooms, though sparsely furnished, were clean and well painted; and the floors were waxed Spanish tile. She could see a television set and other electrical appliances and supposed that since there were no electric wires going into the building or the presence of a wind turbine, somewhere on the premises there had to be a generator or solar panels.

She noticed a small grey wooden building off to the side. It, too, seemed to be well-built and in the same box style. No attempt, however, had been made to make it more appealing to the eye. She supposed that the larger building had once been similarly drab.

The rhythmic beating sounds continued and were coming, she determined, from behind the building. She followed a flagstone path that circled the house to investigate. Turning the corner, she came face to face with Eric Haffner. He looked at her and then at the fence post digger he held in his hands. "It's solid rock," he explained as if he were surprised by the discovery. "I'm wasting my time."

She had never imagined that a conversation with Haffner would begin on such an ordinary note. Drawing on her experience in the convent - where the nuns performed such chores - she replied in the same manner. "You need a miner's pike or drill to gouge out enough stone to fill the hole with concrete so that it can hold the post. Are you building a fence?"

"Yes," he said, propping the post-digger against the wall, "I want to grow vegetables and the animals come out at night and eat everything. Lilyanne, isn't it?"

"Yes." She did not know how to respond in a civil manner. The photographs of her and him together, which she had only glimpsed, now became as clear as portraits in a museum's gallery. "How nice of you to remember," she said sarcastically.

"Don't get nasty. I've thought about you a lot these past two years, and in none of my recollections were you nasty."

"I've thought about you, too. In all of my recollections you are."

"Is that any way to speak to your first lover?"

Instantly, her hand shot out and slapped his face. He touched his cheek and stared at her. Just as spontaneously, an Austrian gentleman surfaced in him. He bowed his head. "I apologize for my crude remark. I forgot that I was addressing a lady. Please forgive me."

She turned and began to walk back to the road. "Don't go!" he called. "It's too dangerous." He quickly jogged up to her and took her arm which she immediately pulled out of his grasp. "It's one thing to come up the road," he said, "but it's another to go down it. The rocks are loose and you'll slide. People have been seriously hurt falling on the road."

She continued to walk. He followed her, pleading. "You can even slide right off it and topple into a crevice. Some of them are deep and spiky. Stay and rest and then I'll walk you down. You're here now. You must have wanted something besides seeing me fail at digging post holes." He tried to block her path. "Please!"

"I don't know what I wanted. It isn't important now. Let me pass."

"You're so much thinner and weaker. I can see that. You've just climbed all the way up here and you're tired. All right. All right. May I follow you down and pick you up when you fall? Then may I bring you up here and give you some tea? Or, can we skip the fall and just have a cup of tea?"

"No." She had reached the road's descent and took a few steps on the loose gravel and rocks. Immediately she felt the pressure on her insteps as her feet pushed against the shoe's laces.

He continued to follow her and then she slipped. She did not fall but she did lose her balance. Her arm flung out for support. Eric grabbed her arm with one hand and with the other grabbed her waist. "I'm not going to hurt you," he said. "But I guarantee that you'll hurt yourself if you don't listen to reason. At least wait until the rain stops. I heard the forecast. It should be over soon." He guided her back to the summit. "You're cold."

"All right," she admitted. "I'm exhausted and thirsty. I don't really have a choice." She went with him to the rear of the building. He opened the kitchen door and asked her to sit at the table.

He filled a pot with bottled water and set it on a butane hot-plate in the kitchen. He put cups on the table. "I have some cookies," he said, "but if you want something more substantial, say the word and I'll make something for you."

"Thank you, but no. Tea will suffice," she said.

The water had not fully boiled when he decided to pour the tea and to sit down to join her at the table. He asked, "Have you seen Henri lately?"

"No. Have I missed much?"

"He's turning into a cupie doll. Charlotte is frantic. Have you seen her?"

"No."

"Then I suppose you don't know that Martin has AIDS. She lives in terror that Martin will infect him. They're lovers."

Lilyanne suppressed a mocking laugh and stared at him. "This is so nice, talking about old friends... old times."

"Don't get sarcastic. Yes, of course, you have every right to act in any way you choose. But I'm hoping you'll be more gracious. After all, in a very real sense, this is your house, too."

"My father's, you mean."

"Maybe he will give it to us for a wedding present. Unlike Henri, I truly do want a wife... and kids."

"You're insane."

"Bored would come closer to what I am. I got bored with the whole Charlotte thing. I started with them when I was only a kid. Did you know that I went to school with Henri in France? I had gotten kicked out of my school in Vienna. I guess my family thought I'd become a very moral fellow if I were exposed to the La Fontaines. Little did they know. I became a remittance man."

"And a criminal."

"Yes... I was in it all the way... and for nearly twenty years. The La Fontaines are an impoverished lot. Michel, Charlotte's husband, had a real title but not a nickel to his name. Did you know that Charlotte's husband was nearly forty years older than she?"

"No."

"Yes. She's from Montreal, you know. She pretends to be a titled noblewoman. There is not an honorable bone in her body."

"I think I know that far better than you," she said, taking a few gulps of tea.

"Yes. That's true. But I can give you all the background information... the personal business - everything you could possibly want to know. AIDS. Remittances. May-December romances. Now that it's all behind me, I can put it into perspective and furnish insightful details. I will be like an open book for you."

"Would you mind if I simply closed the book?" She finished her tea and picked up her tote bag. "Thank you for the tea."

A look of injury passed across his eyes. Closing his book was another way of rejecting him. For an instant he seemed human. She decided to tell him that. "Ah, I offended you. For a nano-second there you seemed to be a human being." She stood up and pushed her chair back to the table.

"I am a human being." He stood up. "Sarcasm does not become you. Since you find me such an objectionable companion, you can walk back down alone." He got up and walked to the sink, keeping his back to her.

Lilyanne smiled to herself. "Ah," she said. "You're actually thinking that I'm going to get all apologetic about hurting your feelings... and tell you I didn't mean it. Well, I did. Thank you for your hospitality."

Eric had indeed supposed that she would so regret hurting his feelings that she'd say something that would make him feel better. He did not move as she opened the kitchen door and crossed the patio to walk down the side path and then to the slippery road.

Lilyanne made it to the first switchback without falling, but as she turned onto the steep and worn part of the road that curved to the opposite direction, she slipped and plopped down on her behind. Her tote back slid from her hand and tottered at the edge of the road, at the top of a crevice, the depth of which she could not gauge from where she sat. Wanting to grab some foliage to pull herself up, she began to inch herself forward but she succeeded only in dragging her bare legs off the protective skirt onto the mud and stones. Suddenly the stress she had contained inside herself for nearly two months burst into a hopeless wail and racking sobs. She did not hear or see Eric come down the road and pick up her tote bag. She was aware of him only when he picked her up and carried her back into the house and laid her on his bed.

"You're shivering with cold. I'm going to put dry clothes on you," he said. She did not struggle when he undressed her and put her arms inside one of his clean dress shirts and used a towel to rub the excess water out of her hair. "I'll make you more hot tea. You need it and then you can rest. You need that, too. You're cold. I have a down comforter. I'll get it for you."

She stopped crying for no other reason but that she was too exhausted to continue crying. She shivered for another ten minutes even after Eric wrapped her tightly in the comforter and continued to hold her as he would hold a child.

Her body seemed to be a mass of conflicting impulses. She wanted to run, to move, to get away, to rest; but her mind was stimulating her muscles beyond their capacity to act. She felt only the frustrated impulses like a thousand tiny electric shocks.

Her wet head stuck out of the top of the wrapping. He laid her back onto the bed. "I'm going to get a hair brush so that your hair will dry." He returned to the bed and began to brush the rain-matted strands of hair. When he finished, he said, "The water's boiling by now. I'll get the tea."

He brought two cups of tea to the bed. "You're like a hot dog in a bun," he said, trying to cheer her. "I like it that your arms are inside and you can't hit me." He propped her up as though she were a swaddled baby and after waiting a few minutes for the tea to cool enough to drink it, he held the cup to her lips and using baby-talk coaxed her into taking a few sips.

"I have peanut butter and crackers," he said, lowering her head onto a pillow. "You need the protein." He went into the kitchen and returned with a tray of crackers, a spreading knife, and a jar of peanut butter.

Lilyanne turned her head away. "I don't want any. Just let me alone. Please, just let me alone."

"All right," he said. "But sooner or later you have to eat something or you won't be able to regain your normal body warmth. Rest awhile in here while your clothing dries."

Gradually the terrible feeling of electricity that seemed to activate every synapse in her body, making her want to move in every direction at once, began to subside as physical fatigue overtook her nervous exhaustion. She began to feel warm again and then her mind drifted into a haze and then, finally, a stupor.

Eric tiptoed into the room and seeing her so oblivious to her surroundings began to tiptoe out of the room, dancing like Rumpelstiltskin or a malevolent elf who had just caught the prized maiden. He could not believe his good fortune. He tiptoed back into the room and picked up her shoes. She would get nowhere without shoes.

He emptied her tote bag onto the kitchen table and, seeing the gutting knife, began to giggle as noiselessly as he could. He took the plastic room key-card and grabbed his wallet and ran to the descending road, slip-sliding his way down a road he had traveled many times.

When he reached the bottom he went directly to the small hotel's registration desk. The clerk knew him on sight. "There was a girl in here looking for you," she said. "She registered."

"Not 'a' girl... but 'the' girl," he said, waving her key-card. "Looks like I'm gonna be an old married man. But right now I need to sign my bride-to-be out before check-out time and she incurs another charge. We've got to watch our pennies." He placed the key-card and some money on the counter. "Does she owe for a restaurant bill?"

"Yes, for a couple of meals. I don't think she left much in her room," the clerk said. "I'll go look."

Eric called, "I'm gonna order some take-out. I'll pay for that separately now." He ordered 2 liters of milk, club sandwiches, an order of German potato salad, and an entire yam pie. "I'll probably be back for dinner take-out, too," he said.

The clerk returned with a laundry bag that contained Lily's soiled garments and shoes. Eric knotted the bag onto his belt. "Need both hands for the food," he said giddily.

"You are really excited. This is the happiest I've ever seen you be," the clerk said, grinning.

"She was late arriving. I was so worried. I thought maybe she changed her mind about getting married. Or maybe something bad happened to her. She's so fragile."

"Yes, I could see that." She presented Eric with Lily's restaurant bill and picked up the money he had put on the counter. He put the change in his pocket.

The food order was prepared. Eric paid and picked it up. "Can't wave goodbye," he called. "No hands! But I'll see you later!"

He whistled as he climbed the slippery path.

Lily was still sound asleep when he returned. He put the containers of milk in an insulated bag he used for a refrigerator and put the rest of the food in the hanging basket. Then he returned to the bedroom and removed his wet clothing and unwrapped Lilyanne enough to be able to get inside the down comforter with her. He feared that his cold body would awaken her, but she was too deeply asleep and did not notice that he was now beside her. Not until he began to kiss her, whispering wildly passionate assertions of love for her and of gratitude to God for bringing them together, did she regain her wits and begin to try to push him away. "What are you doing?" she cried. "Get off me!" She struggled but it was as if each movement she made affirmed his own movements and each protest she made echoed his commitment of eternal love.

"You're mad!" she shouted. "Get away from me!"

"Yes, yes," he exulted, "I know. I've waited so long for you to come to me. God is great! God is good! He will bless us with many children!"

He grabbed her hands and held them up against the headboard. "Every other day I will make love to you," he said with weird excitement. "No matter how often you beg me to make love to you, this once... now... will be all I will give you for today. And not at all tomorrow. But the next day... yes! I can't make love to you more frequently since the old gonads need time to replenish the good little swimmers. This is our moment. You're here and you're about to become united with me eternally. I'll make you pregnant as often as you want." Suddenly he stopped moving.

He looked down at her. "Did you know that the La Fontaines were peasants compared to my family? I wasn't their chauffeur in real life. I was just an actor in the play we were producing. Theater. It was theater. Their houses are like cottages. Wait until you see my family home." He was now seized with an excitement that had nothing to do with her or with what was happening at that moment. He was in another level of consciousness, a deep and fearful area, and his excitement had become maniacal. "I won't ask them to take me back. I'll just show off my well-bred wife and my beautiful son... or daughter. My dear mother will reach out trying to hold her innocent grandchild and then I'll take the baby away and say goodbye. 'Goodbye. Too bad for you. Goodbye'. And then we'll leave and she'll cry."

He giggled about his mother and then he suddenly shifted into a wild sexual enthusiasm and began to babble incoherently and to squeeze his eyes shut. It was as if Lily were a rag doll beneath him with no will or ability to move. She realized that there was no way to stop him and that her part in the intercourse was simply to wait until it had ended. When he finished, he collapsed on the bed beside her, panting from the exertion.

He tried to snuggle with her as she lay there wide-eyed with fear and confusion. He kissed her cheek. "Maybe we can move into your parents' home during the rainy season. It's a quaint little place, but our ambitions are so much less... just healthy kids and good food and lots of love. We'll sail around the Chesapeake Bay in my boat. Did you ever see Remittman? Oh, yes... you did. Last year I saw you there on the pier, watching me. I went down to straighten up the cabin a bit... before I asked you to come aboard. But you left. That fast! You were gone. I called a few hotels, but I figured you were on a cruise ship. I had heard the big horn blow. Henri never even liked you, but I did. I always had a thing for you. You were cute as a button. And now you're mine. And you know... you were probably the reason I fixed this place up. Maybe I knew down deep in my heart that you'd come back to me, that God would finally bless me." He began to play with her hair and to give her little kisses on her head and face. "We have to fatten you up. I brought you lunch."

Lilyanne did not sigh or curse him or inform him that he was insane. She thought that either she was as insane as he was or that this was all part of God's design and she had to accept it without criticism. A peculiar calm enveloped her. "At least the anxiety is over," she told herself. Her heart had begun to beat normally and her hands were not trembling. "Whatever it was that I had feared, it has come to pass."

And then she gulped and ceased to be passive in the events. Frantically she tried to remember what day was the first day of her last menstrual period. It was before she arrived in the Caymans... it had just finished a day before she arrived in the Caymans. And she had been in the Islands eight days.

George returned to his hotel room and checked the recorded events to see all that he had missed at the Williams' house while he had gone to Martinique. He saw the real estate agent show the house to a group of people. He saw them leave and Harriet walk them to the curb.

It grew dark and the camera's images became mostly shadows. He saw a cab's headlights as it parked and Charlotte, as Harriet, wearing deck shoes, get into the cab and drive away. Perhaps she had gone at such a late hour to spend the evening on a boat. But then, two hours later, he saw another cab bring her back to the house. A few hours later, another cab brought Henri - with several suitcases - to the house; and another half hour after that, wearing the same clothes, he departed in a cab.

He saw the real estate agent come back with one of the couples who had seen the house the day before. After they left, the agent returned an hour later to put a "sold" banner across the For Sale sign. Charlotte stood by and smiled as she watched him press the sticker across the sign. "She's sold the place," George muttered. "She has to stay around to close escrow. She won't be leaving before then. But where is Lilyanne? And Henri? And Martin Williams? Williams probably owns the house, too."

He called Beryl and brought her up to date on the trip to Martinique. He told her he wanted to go to the Marina while it was still light and asked her to call Everett to tell him all that had happened. While he was speaking to Beryl, the monitor recorded in present time a cab arriving at the Williams' house and Charlotte going out to get into it. "Charlotte may be going to the marina. If I hurry now I may catch her arriving there. Maybe they've got Lily on another boat."

He got into a waiting cab and went directly to the Marina, arriving moments before Charlotte. He waited for her to pay her driver, and then he followed her. He pretended to be consulting a map so that he could look down and not give her a frontal-face glimpse of him. She stopped beside a large sailing ship which he recognized as the Sesame. A crewman let down the boarding ladder, and, as George continued to walk past her, she climbed aboard. He heard laughter as he passed the ship... congratulatory type laughter. Victorious laughter. He wondered if Lilyanne had been held on the ship all this time... this time that he was looking for her in Martinique. Then he cancelled that thought. Whatever weird things that might have been stowed on the Sesame, a Cuban cellphone was not likely to be one of them.

He stopped in the harbor master's office. "Any word yet on the Remittman?" he asked.

"As far as I know, she's still comin' from or goin' to Jamaica."

Charlotte tried to determine a schedule that would mesh with her plans. She knew that the real estate agent and the title company would do their thing... get the final utility bills, check for liens or encumbrances... and since she and Martin owned the house outright, there would be no delay in bank calculations. She did not want Martin to gain access to an attorney and thereby to draft a new will in which his boy in Namibia would inherit his assets. She told the real estate agent to act with all deliberate speed and agreed to call the utility companies immediately to cut off service to her house and submit a final bill as quickly as possible. She, herself, purchased a large title insurance policy, indemnifying the buyer, and the agent agreed that with the final bills in hand and a search of possible liens filed against the property concluded, escrow could close on Wednesday, February 29th.

She would have to produce Martin for the closing or else get his power of attorney. Everyone knew that he had been sick and that they were a loving couple. It would not arouse anyone's interest to have her represent them both. They'd be relieved that they wouldn't have to sit in the same room with a man who looked as wretched as Martin with all his sagging skin.

But if that were not possible, then she would have to produce him and see to it that the check they received from the sale, as well as his bank account, and the title to the Sesame were all transferred to her. What he could not be allowed to do was to see an attorney. As things stood now, his assets were all willed to Henri. She did not know whether he had consulted another attorney while he was staying with his cousin... but she doubted that he had. As she reviewed their years together she recalled more and more instances of his secretive nature or, what might even be called, his "duplicitous" nature. Perhaps he intended to bring his new boy there from Africa, to install him in another house, or keep him prisoner on the Sesame. She had never seen Martin's will. He had his own safe-deposit box in the bank. As his widow, with a death certificate, she could gain access to the vault and find out. Oh, there were so many "ifs and buts." First things, first. She would get boxes to pack their personal possessions in and take them to the Sesame. Obviously no one could live in a house without water and electricity. She bought a dozen boxes and some packing tape.

At home, she went through her "Harriet" garments and threw everything - except for two dresses, a purse, and two pairs of shoes that she would need for business meetings - into a pile. At the rear of the property she kept a large metal drum with draft holes and a fine screen lid that she could use to burn the garments. She removed all the zippers and plastic buttons and poured a little lighter fluid on the garments and burned them all. The buttons and zippers along with shoes and purses she tossed into the trash can that would be left at the curb.

She had no "Charlotte" garments whatsoever in the house and only a few "Beatrix" outfits which she carefully packed in a box. Even with nearly all of the Harriet garments destroyed, she was still surprised to see how few possessions she had in the house. Most of what she packed were toiletries and a few sets of satin sheets and pillow cases. Things would be different when she was back in France. She would stop in Paris and buy several new outfits. She had thought she'd use the money from Martin's "diamond mine" scam to effect repairs to her home in the

Alpine foothills; but now, she'd have to use Martin's money. And didn't it serve him right!

She called the take-out window of Momma Lotte's restaurant and ordered four containers of spicy shrimp over mashed yams and some Jamaican sweet cakes. She called a cab and had the box and a suitcase put into the car's trunk and then went to the marina via the restaurant's take-out window.

As she called for the boarding ladder to be lowered and looked up to see the cold expression on Martin's face, she knew she was not wanted on the ship.

"What is all this?" Martin demanded.

"The utilities have been ordered to be shut off. I can't very well live in a house that has no water or electricity."

"Can't you find a hotel room?" he asked. "You can't turn this ship into a squatter's camp."

Henri finally objected. "Martin... please... this is my mother! What has gotten into you?"

"I asked the cab to wait for Henri." She turned to Henri. "Darling, I did not want to go through your things to select what you want to keep or what you want to discard. There are empty boxes in the kitchen and a roll of packing tape. Go back now and pack what you want to take to Martinique and what you want to trash. You might want to take Martin with you so that he can do the same... or—" she looked at Martin, "do you want Henri or me to make the decisions?"

"Why don't I go now," Henri said. "It's Martin's meal time. He just took his 'before meals' pills. I see you've brought lunch, so I don't have to go for that now. I'll take Martin to the house to do his packing when I get back."

"I don't need your help to select my clothes," Martin groused.

Henri admonished him. "But you do to pack and move the boxes. Don't be cross!" He pouted and Charlotte had to turn away because the sight of her son pouting like a little girl, sickened and angered her. Henri continued, "We must all cooperate with each other." He climbed down the ladder and went to the waiting cab.

"Where do you want me to stow the box, Darling?" Charlotte asked.

"How long were you planning to stay on my boat?"

She did not answer him. Instead, she asked, "Who else is on board? Just Tommy?"

Hearing his name mentioned, Tommy said, "Just me!"

She gave him money to go to the store and buy a bottle of champagne and some fresh limes and tonic water. She waited until he was halfway down the pier before she turned to Martin and smiled. "I'll take these boxes back, meanwhile, why don't you put the food in the galley."

He followed her into the cabin. She went to the sleeping quarters and put the box on one of the bunks. Then she returned to the galley. "Go wash your hands - you have to be careful not to get any infections! I'll dish out the food."

"I'm not hungry," he said childishly, and he returned to the sleeping area.

She walked back to him, and with an animal's ferocity grabbed his shirt and hurled him onto the bunk. Then she put a pillow over his face and jumped on his body, riding him with her thighs as a jockey rides a horse, holding him down as he flailed the air and made muffled cries.

She released him and as he stared at her with wide uncomprehending eyes, she snarled and hissed, "Now you listen to me, you son of a bitch. Your days of ordering me around are over. Your days of messing with my son are over. I know where your precious Punye lives and I know you gave him AIDS and his parents want to kill you for corrupting him. But I can do much worse to him than they can do to you. I have every letter you two exchanged. You have corrupted a minor child and arrest warrants will be issued for you. And if you deviate in the slightest way from what I tell you to do, he is in for a long and tormented life. I will keep him alive, but I'll sell that beautiful child into sex-slavery and have it tattooed on him that you ordered this to be done. He'll remember you... and every father from the Namib to the Mojave will know what you are. You disgusting pervert! You filthy pig!" She took a deep breath and smiled. "What the authorities in Angola and Namibia are told... what Punye Abados's parents are told... it all depends on how well you obey. Copies of the letters and the charges have been placed in the hands of an attorney who will act if anything happens to me. So pray for my continued good health. What remains of your miserable life depends on it." She got up and stood beside his bunk. "You have a closet filled with clothing that will never fit you again. They will be burned tonight and you will burn them. And you will not let Henri think that anything is wrong... that you fully intend to go through with your plan to live together in Martinique. Is that clear?"

"You are a damnable witch!"

"Idiot... that you didn't know that until now! Now get into the galley and eat!" With these remarks she again grabbed the front of his shirt, pulled him to his feet, and shoved him into the galley.

On the night of February 25th, Martin, Henri, and Charlotte entered the Williams House for the last time. While two cabs waited at the curb, they checked every cupboard and closet, leaving nothing behind for the new owners. Charlotte had even loaded her bicycle into a cab, intending to have it taken to Sesame. Either Henri was going to take what he needed to Martinique, or else he would be giving it to Eric. Martin had surprisingly little to take. He had a few hidden places in the house for papers, but Charlotte had discovered and emptied them. Sullenly, he went out and got into a cab with Henri. "The Barcadere," Henri said, and the cab pulled away.

Charlotte stood at the curb and looked back at the house. "All in all," she thought, "except for the last few months, it was a nice place to live." For a moment she remembered better days with Martin. She sighed. "I am the same now as I was when I was eighteen. My flying jacket. My riding breeches. Everything is the same identical size. How many fifty-five year old women can say that? Why couldn't Martin have kept the faith? Why did he have to backslide into the gutter?"

SUNDAY, FEBRUARY 26, 2012

Eric took several selfie photographs with Lilyanne. Threatening to continue to take photographs until she smiled, he took several pictures of her smiling with her cheek rubbing against his. He bound her wrists to the headboard and ran down the road to the hotel to buy a liter of fresh orange juice, a variety of fresh fruit, butter, and extra eggs. He showed the clerk at the desk the photographs. "She's so shy," he said. "And she was still half asleep!"

He ran back up the road and although he knew that he had bound her well, he was still relieved to see her in the bed. He untied her and allowed her to go into the bathroom alone while he made breakfast. He kept her shoes tucked into his belt.

On Saturday evening he had forced her to eat the club sandwiches and the potato salad. She claimed to be full and would not even taste the yam pie which he left in the basket. But now he put the pie on the patio table. As soon as the tea was ready, he returned to the bathroom and taking her hand, he led her outside into the brilliant morning sun. With a towel he dried off the chairs and ushered her into a seat. He filled the teapot. "Madame will pour?" he asked.

She looked up at him, dumbly. Her expression asked the question, "Who are you?" Her gaze around the patio expressed the same wonderment. She had not yet reached the point at which she would ask herself how she had managed to get herself into such a situation.

Since her hands lay limply in her lap, he moved his chair close to hers so that he could feed her the omelet he had just made. She opened her mouth and began to chew the pieces he inserted.

Breakfast lasted two hours. His manic exhortations of the previous day were gone and in their place he spoke in a rational manner although the thoughts he expressed were delusional.

Clouds had gathered, and in the distance he could see lightning strike. A cloud covered the sun and destroyed his appreciation of the morning meal. "It's going to rain," he said. "Just a shower. It won't last." He cleaned off the table.

Keeping her tennis shoes in his belt, he put the huaraches he had retrieved from the hotel on her feet. "Let's hurry and go look at your new domain." He entwined the fingers of his left hand into her right hand and pulled her to her feet.

He took her to the laboratory. "I ought to clean this out properly, but all these bottles of chemicals might be useful if we find any precious metals on the property. If we don't find anything, I haven't decided what else to use it for. Maybe a music room. I like music. I don't know how we'll get a piano up here - but who knows? By then the road might be paved."

He showed her the mining shaft - which was sealed with an elaborate wooden barricade. "In case you ever want to throw me down the hole, you'll have to take apart that barricade and, frankly, you won't be able to do it. The kids will be safe out here."

A few raindrops began to fall, and he quickly led her into the house. "The office will be our living room. The shutters outside work. You can close them for extra security any time we have a bad storm. And any way you want to furnish it is fine with me." He guided her into the next room. "This room can be the dining room - if you want. You can do anything you want with any of the rooms. Most of the interior walls are not load bearing. They're just partitions. So if you want to remove a wall, just say so. And this room," he ushered her into the entryway, "used to be a waiting room, I guess. But now it can be our humble foyer." Lilyanne, dazed, stumbled along beside him as he showed her the bedrooms. "The biggest one, which of course is ours, used to be occupied by the engineer in charge of the operation. All the smaller ones were used by the men who worked the mine. I combined several small bedrooms to make larger ones. Believe it or not, there were a half dozen small bedrooms! Now there are four... nursery, child, guest, and one for the nanny. Your mom and dad can use the guest room when they come to visit. The kitchen is exactly as it was."

Lilyanne shuffled alongside him, flatfooted, as if she were sleepwalking. She thought that he was truly insane, that he was one of those lunatics who could function in the world - do a job, say 'good morning,' order lunch. Her mind began to clear enough for her to ask herself why she had decided to come to Cayman Brac. She knew that the terms of her new ethics required her to act only after she had thought through the situation and considered all the consequences and then agreed to accept them. She had thought that the worst that could happen to her was that she'd be killed. Where, she wondered, did she get that idea? Had the night terrors and misery she had begun to live through day after day worn down her common sense? Did she think that she could just suspend her natural desire to live until it didn't matter, one way or the other? She had not thought anything through. She knew now that she had acted on impulse and had come to the Islands without a plan or an inkling of possible consequences. "Stupid! Stupid! I figured that by keeping George away I'd be in control of my destiny. Then I had to call him for help. What an idiot I've been. And now... now it may be too late for anything. If I'm pregnant, would I kill my baby's father? Would I kill Eric or any of them anyway? And if George got my message and figured out that I was here, what good would it do if he came after me? I could be pregnant already. George... What an idiot I've been."

Seeing her expression change from wonderment to fear, Eric laughed and led her into the kitchen to "borrow" her gutting knife to slice a melon. "Soon," he whispered, showing her the knife, "I'll have you strong enough to be able to use this thing!"

George did not know whether or not he should believe that Eric had gone all the way to Jamaica. It seemed a little too pat. He had gone to Martinique to check the residence for Lilyanne's presence there. But why shouldn't he check Cayman Brac as well?

He called the airport and asked if he could hire a private plane to show him Little Cayman and Cayman Brac. The two islands were halfway between Grand Cayman Island and Cuba. A slow private plane's flight over each of them would reveal the presence of that "white hulled" ship he had learned about. Any one of a dozen pilots could take him. He asked if anyone knew the place that Claus van Aken bought. Several did, and George selected one who could leave immediately. He hurried to the airport.

The Cessna flew low and George could see the hulls of the few sailing vessels that were in the shipping lane between the islands. None was white. They flew to Cayman Brac and slowly flew over the south coast. The pilot said, "The mines were in the bluffs. That's what Brac means. It's Gaelic for bluff. There are oil rigs in the vicinity, test drilling. There's not much mining of any other kind going on. The one van Aken bought is near the top of the bluffs. A quartz outcrop in the limestone." Slowly they flew over the highest points in the island. The pilot pointed down. "On your right... that tan square building... that's van Aken's place. Doesn't look like anyone's home."

"How can you tell?" George asked.

"Because I can see the harbor and his sloop's not there."

They returned to George Town.

MONDAY, FEBRUARY 27, 2012

For the first time since she had been - in Eric's term - "captivated" by him, Lilyanne was permitted to come into the kitchen to help prepare a meal. Monday was a "love making" day and since she had not tried to hit or kick him, she was rewarded by being allowed to sit at the kitchen table and peel potatoes for hash browns. Then she was allowed to rinse the sand out of fresh spinach.

She was entirely passive now, sunk in hopelessness. Nobody knew where she was, except George. She wondered if he were able to call Captain Quintero back. But surely, by now, she reasoned, George would have figured it out if there were any hint at all of her location. She knew, better than anyone, how clever the "vicious four" were. Tying Claus van Aken together with Eric Haffner would probably be an impossible thing to do without a significant amount of governmental help. They could establish his identity through DNA - providing they had samples. She admonished herself for trying to think. Thinking was what had gotten her into her present situation.

She noticed a spear fishing gun propped up in the corner of the kitchen. Of course, she thought, he must use it to go fishing. She had often seen a fish - with a hole in its side - served to her. Eric noticed her looking at the gun. "Do you have any idea of the strength it takes to load that rubber-band propelled spear into the gun? It will be months before you're ready to shoot me with it."

She did not know how to respond. She remembered Leonardo and his gun belt. "I have seen too many movies," she told herself. And then she realized that she had not seen any movies at all for years. "Or maybe I have not seen enough movies." She closed her eyes and tried to make her vision go blank. When she opened her eyes again, she was looking directly at her own "gutting knife" that lay on the kitchen counter. "How nice of me," she thought, "to have brought him a weapon."

Eric served breakfast: eggs; fried potatoes; spinach; and broiled fish. He had purchased milk from the hotel and served it to her in a goblet. She did not want to eat. He kissed her hand. "Eat," he said. "Do not make me force you to eat. You will only spill food on the floor and draw ants. And you'll still wind up with my food down in your belly."

She ate. Her hand was not trembling as she held the fork. Eric carefully teased the bones from the fish, making sure that she did not eat anything that might harm her. He also had purchased pre-natal vitamins and took great joy in making her take one with her morning tea.

Charlotte stayed with Martin specifically to prevent him from seeing an attorney. Her knowledge of the boy in Namibia was the only leverage she had. She feared that if Henri knew that Martin had a new love in his life, he would respond with maudlin self-pity which would be followed by spiteful hate. It wouldn't go well for anyone. Henri, she decided, was not only becoming more effeminate he was becoming more childish. When she succeeded in getting Martin out of the picture, she would attend to Henri's manliness and temperament.

But what should she do about the money? Since they were tenants in common, two equal checks would be issued. Martin had to be present or else she had to have his power of attorney.

As she left the ship to buy lunch on the wharf, she made Martin and Henri gin and tonics. Henri knew that especially since Martin's gums bled, he should never drink from any glass he was using. She therefore made two drinks: one with an ethanol base and the other normal throughout.

She went onto the wharf and called the real estate agent and in a distraught voice asked what she should do about her husband. She whined, "Martin's not feeling well. His medication is having an adverse effect upon him. We all know that he's normally a wonderful man and that he's anxious to sell the house. We've been happily married for so many years and never had a disagreement. And now he acts like he doesn't know who I am or that I'm his wife or that he ever committed himself to selling the house. Well... you've seen him for yourself."

"Yes, it is terrible," the agent said. "He actually signed the listing agreement."

"If he's considered mentally incompetent then the sale cannot go through. Personally, I think this episode that he's having is a bad reaction to the medicine they gave him in Kingston. But unless we can find a way around his craziness, we'll have to null and void the sale. I suppose it is a valid legal reason to cancel the agreement; but I'd like to see it through. Have you any ideas?"

"Can we get him to assign you power of attorney?"

"I imagine we'd have to do it in such a way that he wouldn't suspect it. He says he doesn't know who I am." She began to act as if she were crying.

The agent, painfully aware that he would lose a substantial commission, thought for a moment and suggested that she come by his office immediately and he'd give her the forms that would convey to her the right to execute documents in Martin's stead. "Perhaps if you appealed to him, he'd see the light and sign the document. We know his signature here in the office and can have it witnessed accordingly. In fact, we also have a notary who'd be happy to notarize it, in case one of the witnesses is out to lunch when you procure the document. We all know Martin and know that if it were not for his unfortunate medical problem, he'd be extremely cooperative."

Charlotte did not place the food order. They would just have to wait. She had more important things to do besides be a servant. She took a cab to the agent's office, picked up the forms, went to the library where she could sit at a desk, took out a copy of Martin's signature which, along with Eric's and Henri's, she had been practicing for years. Authoritatively she signed his name. Then she returned to the agent's office and left the document with his secretary.

She returned to the dock, picked up four lunch platters "to go," and boarded the Sesame. Henri called her aside. "What is wrong with Martin? He's acting strangely... as though he were intoxicated. He won't discuss you or the sale or going to Martinique. He wants me to take him to see an attorney right now, but he doesn't want me to tell you why he wants to go. What is wrong?"

Charlotte knew that the best way to solve a problem was to avoid it. She would not cause any dissension between Henri and Martin until the time was right. "He's getting a reaction to the damp cold. He cannot continue to live on the water. He has to regain his strength and for so long as his immune system is in a weakened state, he can get pneumonia and die. We have to get him off the water. No one is home at Eric's place. Let's get him up there. Let me talk to Tommy and see if he can spend a week or so away from here."

"But won't that interfere with the closing of escrow?"

"That's been postponed for another week but if we should be needed, we can return by plane. Tommy will understand. Call him aside and explain Martin's condition." She watched as Henri took the crewman aside and told him what the plan was. She saw Tommy nod and look at her and wave affirmatively. She walked up to him and said, "Take the wheel." To Henri she said, "Prepare to cast off."

Henri jumped down onto the deck and untied the line which he tossed to Charlotte. Then he jumped onto the boarding ladder and pulled it up after he was safely on deck. The engine started, the ship moved, and as Charlotte saw Sesame separate from the dock, she heard Martin start to shout from his cabin. "Take the wheel," she said to Henri.

She went below, shoved Martin down face-first onto his bed. She grabbed and lifted up his foot, holding onto his middle toe as she plopped down on his back. He could not scream as she twisted his toe. "Shut up you drunken fool." Martin struggled, flailing his arms and other leg. "Hah! You're like a fish on deck flopping around," she said. "As long as I'm holding your toe, you can't do anything because you're too weak." Then she forced his middle toe back until she heard it snap. "Your poor toe is broken. You best stay off your feet."

She released his foot. "All you have to do is to behave yourself and act happy. Escrow will take another week to close. You can go your own way then."

She went up on deck and told Henri to keep Martin locked in his cabin. "It's for his own good. He staggered and stubbed his toe. Now he says that I broke it. Tomorrow we'll be in Brac. He'll start to feel better when he's on dry land."

As they left the harbor, she took the wheel and told Tommy and Henri not to set the sails. "We'll be going only as far as Salt Creek just off Ironshore Drive. "Drop anchor there and wait for me. I have a few things to finish before I join you and we can head up to Brac."

"Aye," Tommy said.

"And never fear," Charlotte added, "I'll pay you for your time and effort. By that I mean, see to it that Mr. Williams stays in his cabin. I'll be getting more medicine for him. He'll be better soon."

TUESDAY, FEBRUARY 28, 2012

It was a day of reckoning for George Wagner. He called Everett Smith who was finally ready to discuss possibilities other than "Rescue."

"I'm going down to the police station this morning," George said somberly, "to see if there have been any more reports of drowning victims or deaths of unknown females. It's time we filed a missing person's report. I know it will be an ordeal for you and Mrs. Smith to be questioned by your local police officers; but be prepared for it. Once the report is filed, you'll be contacted. Can you use your connections to see if the Cuban authorities found anything?"

"Yes, I have someone in the State Department who would know how to find out... and what we should do if they have such a... an... unclaimed body."

"I'll also call Jamaica. If they've found anyone I may have to go there. I just don't know what else we can do. I flew over Haffner's property. He listed it in a commercial name... Goethe Mining. His boat is not there."

"How did you make out when you surveilled the other ship... that Sesame ship?" Everett asked.

"Charlotte, Henri, Martin, and one crewman are on the ship now. It's docked in the Marina. There are food kiosks that serve the ships in the marina. I hung around and saw Charlotte order four dinners to go, and I saw their crewman order four dinners to go. I can't order the police to search the vessel. First of all, Charlotte and company are well regarded hereabouts. Second, I just don't have grounds to even think in terms of their having a girl imprisoned on board... a girl they're starving." George thought, but did not say, that if she were deceased on board, they'd leave the marina and go to sea to dispose of her. A warm feeling of nausea came up from his stomach. "Everett, I've got to hang up now. I'm getting sick. I'll call you later."

As though he were kneeling in a church, George went into the bathroom and knelt before the toilet. The coffee he had earlier consumed came up with a violent urge. It left through his mouth and nose and entered the pine-scented water.

Ten minutes later, he stood up and flushed the toilet. He brushed his teeth and gargled. Then he left to visit the police station and, if necessary, the morgue.

"Before we file the report," Chief Inspector Allan-Royce said, "we ought to check the morgue. They brought another female in last night."

George, white-knuckled with fear, walked beside the Inspector, trying to seem casual. Finally they stood and watched the attendant pull out the drawer in which a female body lay. "She was recovered yesterday," the attendant said, "up on North Beach." He pulled back the sheet far enough for George to see that the woman was definitely not Lilyanne Smith.

He sighed with relief. "No, she's not the girl. But thank you." He turned and walked out of the room. Again, he felt nauseous.

The police officer said, "Then I think we can proceed with filing that missing person's report."

"Let me get some air and then I'll come back," George said, reaching up to hold onto a door jamb to steady himself.

Henri La Fontaine was distressed. "Why," he demanded of Charlotte, "are you treating Martin so erratically? One minute you're nice to him, mixing him a drink, and the next you talk to him as if you're getting ready to make him 'walk the plank.'"

"My moods are governed by his," Charlotte countered. "And do you give me credit for nothing? I'm trying so hard to work things out so that we can all settle our affairs properly. We don't want Martin, in his deplorable mental state, to start hurling accusations that the authorities must at least take seriously. If he's determined to argue, then argue and let him get whatever it is off his chest. Don't even try to talk sense to him. Can't you understand that the man is simply having a reaction to his medication? Give him an opportunity to adjust. It may be necessary for you temporarily to assume control of his assets. His mind is so addled now that he's likely to give everything he's got to some Namibian Orphan Asylum. Really... I don't know what we're supposed to do. We've never had a problem with Martin before." She began to wipe her eyes.

"Tell me what I have to do," Henri said. "I want everything to be finished and running smoothly when we move to Martinique. The house looks wonderful. You should see it."

"I will, my angel, I will. But for now, I'll spend the night on the ship. See to it that some tranquilizers are ground up in Martin's food. In the morning I'll have to take a cab back to George Town. I may be gone another day. I don't know. Bring me all the papers Martin has covering his ownership and insurance on Sesame. Make sure he doesn't see you doing it. Wait until he goes to the head."

Henri hesitated. "Why do you want the papers?"

"Why don't you want to take control of this poor man's property? Do you want someone else to get it through trickery? He said he wanted to live out his life with you. Do you suspect him of lying to you? If you believe him to be honest and sincere, then try to act in his interest. He is suffering now. Whenever it's safe, go and get those papers and his passbook to his account and the key to his safe deposit box and we'll see about keeping his assets out of wily people's hands!"

Henri went into Martin's cabin, and, finding the man sleeping in a drunken stupor, simply opened a secret compartment in which Martin kept his documents and brought her the contents. "I still want to take him to Paris to have him treated. I know that in Paris he will get the care that befits a man of his station."

"Yes," Charlotte murmured. "He is a noble soul and should be treated as one."

George gave the police officer all the information that he had, including the suspicion that she might be on a vessel that had been headed for Jamaica.

"Then let's check with Kingston," the officer said. "They probably do have an unidentified female or two in their morgue. Jamaica is a vacation destination. Tourists flock to the island - same as here. Many like to snorkel and get themselves into trouble while they're recreating. You don't have fingerprint identification or a DNA match. Color of hair: natural blonde. That practically mandates color of eyes: blue. You guess that she's about 5' 2" tall. That's about 157 centimeters. That's about as close to average as you can get around here. Are there any distinguishing marks?"

"Yes," George answered, almost in a whisper. "She has burn scars, neck and foot." He thought that any moment he was going to burst out crying or wailing or doing something that a private investigator ordinarily would not do when making a police report. Trying to end the agony of the impersonal discussion, he said, "Why don't we call Jamaica and see if they've turned up anyone who matches the description?"

The officer made the call. The Kingston authorities said they'd check and get back to him.

"I'll call you at your hotel," the officer said. George, moving like a sleepwalker, nodded and left the station.

Eric had prepared and served breakfast on the patio. He had picked some wildflowers and placed them in a vase at the center of the table. "Flowers for the Lily," he said. She did not reply.

He said, "Shh!" He had heard the sound of a single engine plane in the distance. "Grab your plate and cup and get inside the house!" He picked up his own dishes, but Lily did not move.

"That could be Charlotte," he explained. "She flies her own plane. Get inside the house so that she thinks nobody's home. I hid my boat. I told her I was goin' to Jamaica because I didn't want to get involved with them any more... contrary to your opinion."

"The barbecue fire is lit," Lily said sullenly. "What is the point of going into the house? Do you think she'll assume the neighbors are using your patio?"

They listened to the plane as it passed overhead and continued on until the sound of its engine faded away.

"I ought to turn you over to Charlotte. She'll show you a thing or two about evil."

"Charlotte was only a narcissistic whore. You are an insane rapist."

"So, you finally speak to me and what do you say? Thank you Eric for feeding me? No. You insult me. A little word-sketch for your masterwork? Weaken a few of the ferocious animal's muscles with words... like a *picador*... and then let the star dazzle everyone when she finishes him off with her *estoque*. Maybe you intend to make your first madonna appearance by announcing to your worshippers that your child's father was Satan or something? Kill me with a supreme insult... your matador's sword."

She stared at him. "The bull is a noble animal. It's killed with a noble blade."

He smiled, "Ah, but you did come up here to kill me. I saw the knife in your bag."

"Yes, and it is a pity that I failed. I brought the correct knife... the kind that is used for gutting fish."

"A fragile woman like you should not try to kill a man with a knife, especially after announcing that she intends to do so. If you had the element of surprise going for you, you might have succeeded... stabbed me in the throat."

"Thank you for the advice." She pushed her chair back. "May I please be excused?"

"This is your home. You're not an inmate or a child."

"It's not my home and I am an inmate. I would rather be anywhere else but here."

"Don't act as if you hate me. You don't hate me at all. You saw me a few times wearing a chauffeur's uniform."

"I saw you in photographs... wearing a wig to disguise the coward that you are. I don't know what I was thinking when I came here. I considered killing you because, frankly, you deserve killing. But now I see that you're just pathetic... a sick joke of a man.

"You are right about not punishing the baby if I happen to be pregnant." She got up and slowly began to walk backwards across the concrete patio in her bare feet. "Thank you for telling me about Charlotte and dear sweet Henri and his infected lover. It does my heart good to learn that God has made it unnecessary for their victims to put an end to their criminal careers." She reached for the screen door to pull it open. "That is probably the only good thing to come out of my misbegotten journey here. I can't wait to learn what God has in store for Charlotte."

As she touched the door, his arm moved in front of her, preventing her from opening the door. "Don't make me give up hope for us. I can survive with hope. What did Browning say, 'Man's reach must exceed his grasp else what's a heaven for?'"

"Heaven?" she stared at him. "You really are insane."

At the Lamark Hotel George lay upon his bed, waiting for a thought to occur. Nothing happened. His mind had simply gone blank.

The phone beside his bed rang. As if he were in a dream, he answered it. Everett Smith was calling to say that the Red Cross office was going to check into any unidentified bodies. George could hear Cecelia weeping in the background. "Tell your wife, this is just a precautionary thing that's done. I'm still on the case. I have a feeling that I'd know somehow, someway, if Lily were dead. I don't have that feeling. I only feel the frustration of not being able to find her. Tell Mrs. Smith not to stop praying. This is still a rescue effort for me and it will continue to be a rescue effort until I see her in front of me... one way or the other."

WEDNESDAY, FEBRUARY 29, 2012

Charlotte, looking worried and demure, appeared as Harriet Williams and using the power of attorney granted to her by her husband, Martin Shannon Williams, met in the title company's office with the buyers to close escrow. The couple who purchased the Williams' house paid cash for it, and there were no messy mortgage papers to sign. They asked why Mr. Williams couldn't be present and the title company officer volunteered the information that he personally knew Mr. Williams and had absolutely no doubt about the man's current state of health and of his unconditional desire to sell the house. "He's between two medical regimens," he said with medical certainty. "The old that hasn't worked and the new that has yet to take effect. Mrs. Williams has our sympathy. She has done yeoman's service to assist her ailing husband. We should all have spouses with such incontrovertible loyalty."

With both checks in her hand, Charlotte went to a stationary store and purchased Bill of Sale forms for the sale of the Sesame to her, for the sum of $50,000 and other "good and valuable consideration." She took the form to the recorder's office. Tax stamps had to be affixed to the document. "How much monetary value would you place on that other 'consideration'?" the clerk asked.

Charlotte knew how to make herself appear to be innocent. "I would guess around a million dollars," she said. "It is a very well maintained vessel."

Knowing that her husband had paid less than that when he bought the ship the year before, the clerk smiled. "Let's call it $850,000." She blushed.

With the proper paperwork in her hand, she went to the Registry office and filed the notice of new ownership of the vessel. Asked how her husband was doing, she replied, "He's at a contrary stage. He loves the sea, but pneumonia is such a hazard to him in his weakened condition. And I need not tell you that, no matter where you are, you can get chilled at sea. I'm going to try to get him onto dry land where he can at least look at the sea. His health comes first." She was sad but glad to pay the registration fees for the ketch. Being a resident, she had to pay only a nominal charge.

The bank was equally understanding. She appeared at the vice-president's desk with enough lotion rubbed into her now red and swollen eyes to soften her lids for the next calendar year. The Vice-President was eager to rid himself of a weeping woman. Mourning women did not make a bank look good. He escorted her personally to the vault and had the vault attendant insert the bank's key along with the key that Charlotte had given him.

She went into a private booth and opened the box. As she emptied the contents into a tote bag she had brought with her, she cursed him for his perfidy. Love letters from children. She read a few. They were reminders to keep his promises to them. Jewels. She found an envelope for nearly each of the marriage-blackmail scams they had done. He would go to sell off the stones - which were never reported stolen or lost - and get a top price for them, but he would always keep a few for himself. Perfidy! She thought of Henri as she looked through more of the letters from boys. These waifs had so easily yielded to the attraction of his toni diction and his apparent wealth. "Chicken hawk rogue," she whispered to the box. She counted a dozen flash drives - the complete record of blackmailing photographs - all of which were supposed to have been destroyed! "The beast," she hissed, "intended to use them again, to put us all in jeopardy for his own selfish needs. Damn him!" There were other personal items... gold chains with a meaningful pendant someone had given him... watches he had taken from young women in the marriage-blackmail scheme. He had told her that he fenced them. Why had he kept them? "Huh!" she growled. "He would give them to boys to get them to act like girls. That kind of perversion appealed to him." She decided that his death should not be a pleasant one.

She left the empty box in the private booth and opened her own safe-deposit box and removed a dozen velvet boxes that contained a variety of jewels and other heirlooms. Then she went to the teller's window to close their respective accounts, asking if she could receive the money in U.S. dollars since she and her husband were going to live with a sister in Atlanta, Georgia. In a special cardboard box the teller stacked nearly $400K from Martin's account and nearly $4K from Harriet Williams' account.

She looked at her watch. It was just noon. It had taken her two hours to gain the fruits of Martin's decades of criminal labor. "It is little enough," she decided. "Without me, he would have died a pauper."

The cab took her north on West Bay Road and turned off on Green Leaf then Yacht Drive, and finally Ironshore Drive. She could see The Sesame anchored at Salt Creek. She called Henri and he came to her immediately in the dinghy. As they approached the ship, she threw the dozen flash drives into the ocean. She boarded the ship with all the documents that Martin had thought he could conceal from her. "Set a course for Cayman Brac," she told Tommy, but it was she who took the wheel while Tommy and Henri began to raise the sails. Since the wind was striking them on the port side and Charlotte was feeling particularly ebullient, she called, "Hoist the spinnaker!" and Henri and Tommy raised the huge nylon sail with the Aladdin's lamp painted on it. The Sesame's prow sliced the water with its chest proudly out, as the great sail caught the wind and billowed triumphantly.

Eric, still smarting from the insults he had received the day before, tied Lily to the bed as he prepared to go fishing. "Previously I worried. I asked myself what would happen to you if I were killed by a shark. I'd be in heaven before you; but I'd wait. It would take you a few days to die. Now I'm not worried. It's Wednesday. A love making day. Your cycle is coming to a close. This will be the last day I come to you for love. You'll be captured by hate until another month passes... unless my swimmers have done their job. And then in a couple of weeks things will be different. No more hate. So this morning I'll be in cold water. The swimmers like cold water. Be prepared for their little contest when I get back."

He returned in an hour and brought the beautiful iridescent mahi mahi he had speared into the bedroom to show her. "Look! The storm must have driven the fish in to shore!" He took the fish into the kitchen and put it on the sink. He returned to the bedroom and began to undress. "First you and my swimmers, and then I'll gut the fish." He did not tell her that he had stopped at the hotel to tell the clerk he'd be bringing two-thirds of the large fish back to them as a gift after he showed the fish to Lily. The clerk then called him aside. She wanted to know if his bride-to-be would like a kitten. People who lived on their boat kept a cat that delivered a litter of kittens a month before. The kittens were left at the hotel for the clerk to give to anyone who wanted one. Eric took a little orange colored female. He left it in a box out on the patio.

As he got into bed with Lily, he asked, "Did you miss me?"

Eric Haffner's excitement and his irrational interpretation of events settled into more realistic levels. "Come outside and sit on the patio. You need the sunlight." She did not want to leave the bed, but he pulled her up and marched her outside. "Sit on the long chair and say, 'Eric, you are really very nice to me and I love you for it.'"

"I would sooner cut my tongue out," she said.

He opened the box and the kitten climbed out.

"Ahh!" Lilyanne squealed. "Where did you get it?"

"That is not what you are supposed to say. Tell me you love me or I'll let it run off into the jungle, and I guarantee it'll be dead in half an hour."

He trailed a length of fish gut across the patio and the kitten followed it. "I'll count to five. If you don't say it then, I'll throw the gut into the bush and it'll follow it."

She got up and went into the kitchen and put her head on the table and began to cry, sobbing a prayer.

He came in, carrying the kitten. "Here, you bitch," he said, putting the kitten on the table. "You win this round. But trust me, my girl, you will not win them all."

He took a machete and cut the large fish. "I'm taking the fish down to the hotel. We can't eat it all, and it would only go bad. Use your gutting knife and mince a little piece for the cat."

He had grown weary of trying to communicate with her. All the way down the hill he talked to himself. She had not spoken two congenial words to him since Saturday. In fact, as he strove to recall, the only nice words she had said to him at all were words of advice on gouging out holes in which he could set fence posts. Other than that she had either insulted him or had responded with sullen expressions or scathing sarcasm. He decided that the time had come when they had to reach some kind of detente.

"See here," he said, when he returned, "you need to be more civil to me. You should look forward to our attachment. We will be parents together."

"Attachment?" she said.

"Nuptial attachment. You would want your child to have a father. Many women get pregnant and cannot even force the man to marry them. Here am I, begging you to be my wife as well as the mother of my children. You will be my hostess. Wouldn't you like to be Madame Haffner?"

"I would sooner throw myself into a pool of lampreys."

Eric laughed. "Lampreys! Excellent. Thank God you picked that Cuban ship! I am so tired of stupid women. You can be the slave and I will be your Emperor Augustus. I will save you."

"You missed the point. I would willingly go into the pool and be attached to a thousand sucking lampreys than be attached to you on dry land."

"Would? Why do you say 'would'? We're already attached. And in less than a week, I've even managed to put some weight on you. You look better today than you did last Saturday. Would you have done as well on your own?"

"Away from you, I would have done better if I found myself lying on an embalmer's table."

He scowled. "That's a poor choice of words after I brought you the gift of a kitten. But you would never put yourself on such a table if you had an innocent child inside you. So let's talk about more pleasant things." He pulled a chair next to hers. "Let's have tea. Sun tea. Do you like sun tea? Do you even know what it is?"

"No."

"You take a clean gallon jar like this and fill it with bottled spring water." He emptied several bottles of water into the jar. "Then you add a ball-strainer filled with good quality tea... Darjeeling, I like best." He filled the ball-strainer and submerged it in the water. Immediately amber color diffused through the water. "Then you screw the top on and put the water in the sun. God does the rest.

"While we wait we can sit here and discuss names. What would you like to name our baby?"

"A Christening?" She suddenly saw herself holding a baby in its sacramental raiment... a long lace gown... godparents at the ready. Who? George, surely. Beryl. Yes, Beryl. Was Beryl a Catholic? That she would be asking herself such a question became a reality she could not understand. The abyss again opened and her emotions began to fall down, down, down until her forehead touched the table and she began to sob again - not hysterically, but in a manner, *de profundis*, in wails that seemed to come from beneath her lungs.

Eric Haffner saw and heard her agonized cries and tried to comfort her. He moved his chair beside hers. "Don't you see that I can't let you go? You're all there is between me and a terrible end. I will never survive alone. I need to be justified, to be reborn."

She stopped crying and looked up at him to see a single tear roll down his cheek. She turned away again and let her forehead rest on the table. "Oh, my God," she whispered. "Oh, my God, why have you abandoned me?" The kitten began to play with her hair.

"Go to hell," Eric said softly as he stood up. "Stop crying. If you don't do as I say, I will whip your delicate feet until they bleed. And then I'll be able to stand back and watch you crawl to me for food and drink."

He thought he heard his name being called. "Shh!" he said, touching her shoulder.

"Eric!" Charlotte called his name again. He went to the front of the house and saw Charlotte, in her adventuress "Beatrix" guise, coming towards him. "What are you doing here?" she asked.

"I live here," he answered. He quickly turned back to Lilyanne. "Charlotte is here. Go into the bedroom and behave yourself. Take the kitten with you. If you act nasty I'll turn you over to her. If she sees you, act like you're here because you want to be!" He called to Charlotte, "Come around to the back."

As Charlotte walked around to the rear of the building, Lilyanne put cold water on her face and, carrying the kitten, walked back into the bedroom.

Charlotte stood on the rear patio and admired the house. She looked through the kitchen's screen door and noticed two tea cups on the table. "I like what you've done with the place. But you're supposed to be in Jamaica... or on your way back from there. The Remittman is nowhere around. Have you hidden her somewhere?"

"Obviously. I wanted some privacy."

"We'll be out of the way sooner than you think. Do be an angel and help Henri to get Martin up here. I've got a wonderful proposition for you. We're free and clear of the Caymans. I now own everything that monster owned. And I'll split it with you... or give you the Sesame outright for your help. I have soooo much to tell you."

"Why have you brought Martin here?"

She pulled Eric away from the kitchen entrance, and in a low voice, she said, "I had to get him away before he consulted an attorney. He's so enamored of this other boy... the one in Namibia."

"Is Henri at the bottom of the hill?"

"Yes. Who's in the kitchen with you? Playmate? Housekeeper? Well, why don't you 'secure the help' and come down and give us a hand with

Martin. Henri doesn't know about Martin's duplicity, so don't say a word about it."

"The 'help' is my wife; and we think she's pregnant so I definitely do not want Martin up here. God damn it, Charlotte. I bought this place to get away from ugly things; and here you are - without an invitation - coming here with a diseased man."

"Your wife? When did you get married?"

"Technically we're not married yet. She's someone you know. Do you remember Lilyanne Smith?"

"Oh, the one with that intolerable mother. She's here? Well, congratulations, dear."

"It's a serious relationship we've got, and that's why I don't want you depositing trouble on my doorstep."

"Eric! Please don't be angry. I didn't think you were here! I'm sorry! But the dissolution of our business has been dumped on my shoulders. Can you not at least cooperate? This is our last official act together. Please, let's finish this amicably! I've been through so much lately. Help Henri to get the bastard up the hill."

"I told you already that I don't want him touching anything of mine. Why the hell did you bring him here?"

"Until you and I can come to some accord about disposing of the son-of-a-bitch, I'm stuck with him. I need to get rid of him in a way that won't hurt Henri. Martin can't walk."

"Why not?"

"Because I broke his toe. I had to keep him from seeing a lawyer!"

Eric sighed. "Jesus, is there no end?" He relented. "All right. But I'm not doing your dirty work for you. Don't even think about it. I don't want him opening his big mouth down at the hotel. Just understand that I'm not going to touch him. I have a wheelbarrow. It's big. We can cart him up in it."

"All right. I personally don't give a damn if you drag him up here by his heels." She paused. "Henri is so confused. Martin's been so erratic lately. Sane one minute. Crazy the next. That ethanol stuff is wonderful. I threatened to tell the boy's parents about him so he's playing along with the idea that he and Henri will be moving to Martinique. He thinks we're waiting here for escrow to close and then he'll go to meet up with his boy. He wants to hire a few sailors and sail the Sesame to South Africa. He doesn't know escrow's already closed and that I've got everything he owns. He's not going anywhere. Eric, I don't want him living with my son in Martinique; but if Henri learned the truth about Martin's new love, it would kill him. We have to finesse this ending. Please help me."

Eric went to the lab which he used to store tools. He pushed the wheelbarrow out and told Charlotte to take it and start down the hill while he attended to an old bed that he had in the lab. He called to Lilyanne, "Lily, would you bring me a couple of sheets, a pillow and pillow case? I'm going to fix the bed in the lab. Martin is coming up and I'd prefer it if he slept in here. AIDS is not the only disease he had." He turned to Charlotte. "Go ahead! I'll get a place ready for him in here."

As soon as Charlotte started down the hill, Lilyanne brought the bed linens to the lab and helped him to make the bed. When they finished, Eric looked at her. "Thank you for the help," he said, "and would you please go inside the house. There is a bed there; and if you don't try to sneak out of it, I won't tie you to it. And don't let the kitten near her. Her disposition is contagious."

He went down the hill to help transport Martin.

The windows were open and Lilyanne could hear the shouts to be careful and the laughter that followed near disasters. Finally, at the top of the hill, the wheelbarrow was pushed onto the rear patio. It had been exhausting work and Charlotte, Henri, and Eric all collapsed onto chairs.

"Get me out of the sun!" Martin shouted, and Henri got up to help him to get to his feet. "My cane!" Martin groused; and Charlotte, who had carried the cane up the hill, took it to him, saying under her breath, "Watch your mouth before you end up down a mine shaft!" Then she smiled, "Here it is, Darling. Let me get the kitchen door for you."

They went into the kitchen. Henri poured Martin a glass of sun tea and asked if he wanted to sweeten it himself. Martin nodded and put half a dozen sugar cubes into the drink. As he stirred it, he said, "Are you gonna wait on me like this when we're home in Martinique?"

Henri gave a simpering response. "No. When we're in Martinique you'll be so strong that it will be all I can do to keep you from waiting on me... and on the cook... and on Samuel. Why, everyone will come up from Saint-Pierre to watch you cut down trees and hurl boulders into the sea."

Charlotte stood up and spoke to Henri. "We have personal valuables on board the Sesame with only Tommy standing guard. Let's leave Martin up here with Eric - they can talk about old times - while we go and get our jewelry."

Lilyanne said nothing while she listened to Eric talk about the house... the bedroom that would become the nursery... the sturdiness of the construction. "It is hurricane-proof," he boasted.

At noon, Henri, carrying food he had purchased at the hotel, and Charlotte, carrying velvet boxes of jewelry and heirloom items that belonged to her husband's "lineage," approached the house and entered it through the kitchen door in the rear.

The food was deposited on the kitchen table and the jewelry boxes on a shelf of a side cupboard. Eric brought Lily's dinner into their bedroom and fed it to her, wiping her mouth and chin as though she were a baby. When he finished, he took the dishes into the kitchen where Charlotte waited for him to discuss something "in private."

They came out the front door and stood so close to the master bedroom's window that Lilyanne could clearly hear every word they said.

"I have a proposition for you," Charlotte began. "For reasons, some of which are obvious, I cannot let this romance continue between Henri and Martin. My son is so devoted to that miserable fool. Martin spent company money going to Angola for the diamond-mine scam. He did nothing about the scam, but what he did do was run wild with his skank friends and get himself diseased. AIDS, gonorrhea, and God knows what else. He went into Namibia and, hungry as usual, he searched for his personal buffet, a private school for boys. You know how Martin can charm young boys." She produced several letters from her skirt pocket.

"Here are some love letters from children that Martin put in his safe-deposit box."

"Jesus," Eric said. "These are all written by kids."

"High school kids... fourteen... fifteen." She selected one of the letters. "This one is from the Namibian boy."

Eric read the letter to himself. "He really has snowed this kid. And this is the one he gave AIDS to?"

"Yes. This is the kind of snake we're holding next to our hearts. I'm beside myself with worry. You know that he'll inherit property from Henri. Henri owns that house in Martinique. I am not exaggerating when I tell you that it wouldn't surprise me if he intends to do away with Henri just to get a nice little love-nest for his new boy." She began to cry. "Eric... please help me. Henri believes in him and the more Martin mistreats him, the more he tries to please him. My son is not well... not emotionally. I have got to get him away from this monster before he destroys him physically, too."

"How does this concern me?" Eric asked.

"Because of Martin's condition, I now have his power of attorney. Yesterday I closed on the house and got both checks for $450K. I also emptied his bank account of $400K. His safe-deposit box had some nice jewelry in it - that I didn't even know he had. And, of course, I sold myself the Sesame. The boat is already listed with the Maritime Registry. I'll give you the Sesame in exchange for the Remittman and I'll also give you $400K in cash from the house plus another $200K cash from his bank account. And if you see any jewelry in the pile that you'd like, take it. In return, I want you to take Martin and me down to George Town and on the trip he will choke on a bone. As you will explain it to the authorities, 'She was bringing Martin to his physician for new treatment. He had smelled the fish that we were having for lunch and wanted to eat it. He was such an independent soul that he refused to allow Harriet to cut the fish and examine it for bones. And just like that, he choked on a bone. We didn't hear anything because we were on deck... tacking, adjusting the sails... and when we returned to the galley, he was on the floor and had evidently choked to death.' I will be unable to speak since I'm so grief-stricken; and you, you're appalled that such a thing would happen to your old friend - and on your boat, yet! Even a cursory examination by a physician will reveal the clogged fish in the dead man's throat. His physical condition will be daunting to any pathologist. I don't see them even ordering an autopsy. Are you in?"

"I have to think about it. I had hopes that having a respectable woman live with me would help me to live a better life. I was tired of all the games. But I've come to the conclusion that I'm just trying to trade guilt for scorn. I've had enough scorn in my life. But all I've done is find an honorable way to get the same old bullshit. So, let me think about it."

Lilyanne bit her lip listening to him. "So now because I was mean to him, he's going to commit murder? He *had* changed for the better. He's mentally sick and yet he put that life of crime behind him. Have I caused him to fall back into it? Dear Lord! Because I had to be so self-righteous and nasty, I've made him reverse his salvation. Am I responsible for damning him... by causing him to commit a mortal sin? What have I done?" She began to pray for forgiveness. At the end of the prayer she asked, "Lampreys? Why did I have to bring up lampreys?"

Alejo Quintero received a call from the security department of both CUBACEL (Cellular Telephone of Cuba) and C-COM (Caribbean Cellular), asking him to stop by Juan delMonte's office on Tuesday morning.

Quintero and delMonte were old friends, distant cousins, in fact. They exchanged the usual pleasantries and Quintero told him he had visited his son in prison. He did not mention that both of Francisco's front teeth had been knocked out - a frequent initiation into the exclusively male sex of any prison. "I'm going to see to it that he has good books to read and a little inspirational stuff too. His mother says we neglected his -" he paused to affect a sly look - "religious education."

DelMonte laughed at the little joke. "I suppose you can take comfort in the fact that kids all over the world are the same. If you have three sons, you're lucky if two are average, and only one is a fool. Most men raise three fools."

"Tell me why daughters are such joy until they meet one of those fools," Quintero smiled. "What can I do for you, today?"

"I know it's probably nothing," delMonte said, "but you made a call to the United States a week ago." He pushed the telephone call record across his desk for Quintero to see it. A line in the bill was highlighted. "Can you tell me why you made the call?"

"I made no such call. Who got it?" He read the line which included the name of the person called, the number, time and duration of the call. "George Wagner? The call was less than a minute. It could have been a wrong number."

DelMonte prided himself on being able to detect a lie. He could detect no deceit in Quintero's response.

"Wait a minute," Quintero said. "I've heard that name. But I didn't make the call. He looked at the bill and noted the number called. Perhaps when I was at lunch with my jacket on the chair... I don't know... I'm guessing... there were young people at the next table. Maybe one of them played a joke and called the number. Check with Hugo Azuela. He and I were in the restaurant at the same time... which was, I see, just around the time this call was made. Maybe he saw something."

"It seems to be a joke. The call was less than a minute."

"I should have been more careful with my phone. I'll just pay the bill. I won't dispute the charge on the bill... unless it's important and you want to investigate further."

"No. They probably didn't plan a revolution in less than a minute's time." He laughed, and Alejo Quintero, who suddenly did remember where he had heard the name, laughed with him.

Quintero went to see Ivan Rostov, one of the Russian businessmen who frequently came to Cuba. Rostov was one of a group of foreigners who, along with a few Cuban administrators, regularly put sums of money into bank accounts in the Cayman Islands. They would give Quintero the cash and their passbooks in a sealed envelope, and twice a month, he would sail the 275 miles to George Town and deposit the money into their accounts. There were no electronic transfer records indicating that the transactions were from any foreign point. When they wanted to withdraw the money, they gave him the passbook and a note in pencil of the sum they wanted. He would withdraw it and give them the passbook and the money.

Quintero, considering the performance of his service as a means to redeem the slur placed upon his name by his son's trial, performed the task with ease. The only difficulties he encountered were with counterfeit currency. In the shipment in which Lilyanne had become a stowaway, no less than three of the deposits he was to make contained counterfeit notes. The bank retained the bad notes and gave him documentation to that effect. The depositors were always disappointed and placed in the position of trying to determine where they had gotten the counterfeit money. Quintero's honesty had been tested several times and each time his accounts of the difficulty had proven to be accurate. Regarded as a completely trustworthy courier, he remained scrupulously honest performing transactions that were far from ethical.

Ivan Rostov, one of the Russian businessmen who used Quintero's courier services, was told that the captain wanted to see him on a private matter. He, as well as all the others, always feared that Quintero, knowing how much money he had in the bank, would ask him for a loan. He was therefore pleasantly surprised to be asked if he could use his cellphone to make a call that would not be appearing on any local invoices. The businessman happily gave Quintero his phone. A secret number like this was leverage in case Quintero ever got any ideas about his money.

George's cellphone rang. He leaped to get it. "Wagner here," he said quickly.

"Wagner, you don't know me, but a girl hid on my ship and managed to use my cellphone to call you. I have a Cuban phone."

"Yes," George said, "I got the call. Lilyanne made it. Is she all right?"

"She was the last time I saw her. A little bit thin but strong in her mind. Last Friday, I took her where she wanted to go... to Cayman Brac."

"Why was she with you? I don't understand."

"She was a stowaway on my ship. Actually, she was just visiting with a young man who guards the ship when I'm doing business in George

Town. I returned to the ship early and angry. Some of the money I was going to deposit - British pound notes - turned out to be counterfeit, which is, in a manner of speaking, a royal pain in the ass. I ordered my crew to cast off and by the time I finally cooled down, we were in Cuban waters. She and I had a nice conversation and she mentioned your name - she said you had rescued her once from the problem that had brought her to the Caymans. She was looking for one of the guys who had extorted her father and hurt her. Just this afternoon I got asked by the security service why I called the United States. I didn't call the U.S. and thought it must have happened when I was having lunch in town. I was shown the bill and noticed your name and number but I didn't make the connection right away. She never mentioned using my phone. I guess she was too afraid to tell me. I borrowed a friend's cellphone to let you know. I thought you might want to know that I dropped her off in Cayman Brac."

"Captain, you have my deepest thanks for taking the trouble to tell me. I'm down here in George Town, looking for her. I'll go up to Cayman Brac as soon as possible to see if she needs some help. Again, many thanks. *Muchos Gracias.*"

Quintero laughed. "It's '*Muchas gracias,*' and you're very welcome."

George disconnected the call and took the first deep breath he had had in days. He checked his watch. It was after five o'clock. He made a quick call to Everett Smith who wanted details which George could not supply. "I'm calling the private plane airport to see if I can get a flight up there. It's been raining at night and I know they won't fly in the evening if conditions aren't perfect."

He called the airport and was told that the earliest flight he could get would be at 9 a.m. the following morning. George made the reservation.

Eric could not resist showing his bride to his former friends. He brought her into the kitchen and put his arm around her, making sure that no one got too close. Kissing her on the cheek, he said, "You run along and hop into bed and get some rest. It's not good for you to stay on your feet too long." He walked her into the bedroom.

Lilyanne heard them laughing in the kitchen. Eric had opened a bottle of champagne. Martin had begun to speak to Henri with considerably more respect. As Charlotte interpreted his sudden cordiality, Martin had begun to suspect that she and Eric were plotting against him, hoping that with him out of the way, they could get their hands on his money and ship. No doubt he had realized that Henri's love for him would function as an insurance policy against any of their actions against him. She smiled at the man's stupidity.

Martin did fear that they'd try to disrupt his plans for Namibia. He also needed time to regain his strength. There was no better place to do this than in Martinique. When he was ready, he'd leave the irritating Henri, hire a few sailors, and take the Sesame to Sierra Leone and then sail down the coast of West Africa to Angola. He wouldn't hazard entering Namibian waters. Who knew what his vicious associates would do out of jealousy and contempt? He could communicate with Punye through friends. Meanwhile, that he still had the idiot French nobleman under his thumb was, apparently, cause for celebration. He therefore drank a toast with Henri. "To life in Martinique!"

Hinting that she had something sexual in mind, Charlotte took Eric's arm and slyly said, "Let's let these two birds talk about the future while we go off and recall our own old times." She led Eric out the front door and stood in front of the same bedroom window.

"How did you get hooked up with the Smith girl?" Charlotte asked.

"She came down trying to kill me."

"And you love to watch the competition."

"There was no competition. For once, not a single female was pursuing me with murder on the brain."

"Except me!"

"Come on, Lady. You don't pursue anyone. You set traps."

"Maybe with her on your arm you can go back to Europe. Your family will check her out and as I can tell you, their wealth is substantial and they're quite legit."

"I was hoping that she'd see things that way. But she's like an oak tree. She won't bend."

"Are you sure she's pregnant?"

"No. I'm just hoping she is. I'm doing my best. Once every other day."

"That's right. Give the boys time to assemble." She nudged him playfully. "Have you given my proposition any thought? I'm not trying to rush you, but I thought of a good way to get Martin to leave quietly."

"What's that?"

"He's due to take his after meal capsules now. I've hidden one of the new bottles. I'll say that it must have rolled off the edge of the road while we were coming up here. I did drop a few things. The bloody road is too slippery. Anyway, he's got enough to keep him on his medicine cocktail for three more days. But he'll have to return to George Town to get the missing bottle replaced and, of course, to attend the escrow meeting."

"If we do away with Martin on a trip to Grand Cayman, how will we keep Henri here? He can't be with us."

"Well, Martin's only making a show of being nice to Henri. He'll want to get away from him. He'll help to convince Henri that he should stay behind and look after your bride. We'll take the Remittman because it's faster. Tonight we'll just have to keep things congenial."

"I don't want him sleeping with Henri - not inside this house!"

"All right, then. Be supportive when I tell Henri that if he wants to get anything out of this romance he has to play by the rules. Martin has to get better and he can't get better unless he gets new medication. So he'll have to stay behind to guard the girl while Tommy stays on board the Sesame. How long do you think it will take?"

"It depends on the wind. Guess a day and a half to get there... another day of Coroner's paperwork... maybe two days... and then we can return... a day. Five or six days total. Can you leave Henri alone up here for that long?"

"He's not a helpless baby!"

"Yes he is, Charlotte. I'm not gonna comment on your parenting skills, but I hope to hell mine are a whole lot better. He's half nuts with all these romantic demands made on him. When you get back to France, get him some therapy."

"Let him tell a psychiatrist everything he's done?... *we've* done? Are you out of your mind?"

"Right. Well, maybe you can effect some kind of catharsis. Get him to write romance novels."

"You fool!" she playfully teased him. "I want him to be more masculine... not another Bronte sister."

"You've got all that Alpine ice. Give him a hockey stick."

They both laughed. Eric tugged at her waist. "I'll have to watch Martin. I don't want him using my bathroom or going any place he feels like going. The man has no regards for anyone else's welfare."

Charlotte took out a pack of cigarettes, lit one and leaned against the wall. She could see the ocean from the front of Eric's house. "It won't be long now," she assured Eric. "You're already set right here and I've got only one more ocean to cross and I can enjoy life having a salon... a nice apartment in Paris where important people like to come to my 'at home' evenings. Henri will be able to meet a rich girl and, who knows, I may also meet someone who excites me."

Eric mussed her hair. "I wish you better luck with love than I'm having." He turned and walked around the house to the patio outside the kitchen. "Where's Martin?" he asked Henri. "I don't want him using my toilet facilities. There's a small outhouse by the laboratory."

"Don't treat Martin as though he were a leper," Henri said.

"I'd be less afraid if he were a leper," Eric countered. "Where is he?"

Henri got up and shoved the chair back against the table. "Well! I'll go make sure he's not using your sacred toilet!" He smelled tobacco smoke coming from the master bedroom. The door was open and he walked into the room. He did not see Charlotte outside smoking a cigarette and exhaling the smoke which the breeze carried into the bedroom.

He looked at Lilyanne who was still quietly staying under the sheet, playing with the kitten. "When did you take up smoking?" he asked.

"I didn't," Lilyanne answered. Outside Charlotte heard their voices so clearly that she knew Lilyanne had heard every word that she and Eric had spoken. One thing became immediately certain: Lilyanne could not leave Eric's place. She dropped her cigarette and crushed it with her foot, cursing Eric for having been so careless. He knew the layout of his own home. He never should have engaged in such a conversation, knowing that someone was a few meters away.

It was Martin's after-meal time to take his pills. Charlotte made a convincing show of not being able to find one of his new bottles of capsules. "Well," she said, "that settles it. We'll have to go back to George Town. We had to go anyway to close on the house sale; but now we'll just have to go a day or so sooner."

"I have a few more things to pick up," Eric said. "We can take Remittman. It's faster and all that tacking on Sesame is too goddamned laborious."

"We'll stay in a hotel," Charlotte insisted. "Sleeping on the water is not good for Martin."

Martin did not object. This was his opportunity to see an attorney.

It came as no surprise to Lilyanne that Eric came to the bedroom after dinner and announced that he was taking her to the laboratory. "Someone who appreciates me will be using this bed with me. And you can sleep in the laboratory." He was carrying a cup of milk and a little bag of minced fish. "To show you what a nice guy I really am, I've brought some food for the cat."

They walked together across the gravel area to the lab. But once they were inside the building, he bound her hands behind her and wrapped her ankles, using duct tape that he had brought from the bedroom. He also took her shoes so that even if she were to free herself she could not walk barefooted across the sharp gravel that lay between the lab and the house and also between the lab and the path down the hill. He covered her and said he'd be in again in an hour or so to make sure he had not bound her too tightly. He left the roll of tape on the workbench.

Lying on the cot, she could hear the convivial laughter. If she had been civil to Eric... more Christian towards him... maybe he would not have agreed to help Charlotte. That responsibility was hers. Now they were going to kill someone. God would know what they had done. And she was complicit in the act. Were it not for her sarcasm and nastiness, her total lack of compassion for a man who was obviously mentally ill, Eric would have one less mortal sin on his soul. But, on the other hand, what about her mission? The only evil that was about to end was Martin's. But one way or the other, he wouldn't be infecting anyone else. Martin was no longer in the picture. Henri would go on to be the sociopath that Charlotte was. "Everything is so enormously complicated!" She began to cry. "George," she whispered. "Why didn't I just talk things over with you? George. My sweet George…"

The kitchen lamps were lit. Charlotte was talking about the heirloom jewelry. Lilyanne put her feet on the floor and tried to stand up and hop to the window. She could not balance herself and had to lean against the wall. She could see into the kitchen. Charlotte was showing off gold cufflinks her husband had gotten from his father. "The family crest is engraved on them," Charlotte was saying. "They are Henri's pride and joy, his emblem of ancestry."

Henri, sounding like a girl, proclaimed, "Next to Martin, I love these precious reminders of my lineage." The cufflinks were in a red velvet box that had a spring closure. As the lid clamped shut, the word "engrave" stuck in Lily's mind. The kitchen door opened and Eric started to come back to check on her. She hopped back to the bed.

"Is this too tight?" he asked, tugging at the tape around her ankles.

She did not want him to remove the tape that was on the workbench. "No, it's all right. Eric," she said, "I'm sorry I said those mean things to you about lampreys. I know you mean well. I don't know what got into me. I'm really sorry I was so mean."

Surprised, he sat on the edge of the cot and looked down at her. "You should be sorry. That was a terrible thing to say to someone who only wants to love you. All right. I'll still try to be your Augustus." He kissed her on her nose and cheek. "You be a good slave and don't break any glassware. I'll try to get rid of them as quickly as I can." Then he asked, "How's the kitten? Did you name her?"

"Yes. She's sleeping now. I've named her Brynhilde."

He laughed. "Our first little Valkyrie." He bent over her and kissed her cheek. "Are your wrists ok?"

"Yes, they're fine. Can you leave a little light on in here so that the bugs won't come out?"

"Sure," he said. "How about if I light a candle? The drawer's full of 'em."

"Thank you. But make sure it's stable. I don't want it to fall over and set the place on fire."

"Yes, Mother," he teased. "I think I know how to make a candle stable." He found a hurricane lamp. "Here, I'll put it in under the glass and you'll be safe even if there's a wind tonight."

He left the lab and walked to the house. She heard the kitchen's screen door open and shut. And then she heard him throw the bolt.

How could she create dissension in the group? Maybe if they fought they'd give up their plan to kill Martin. Maybe they'd even attack each other. But how?

Nothing came to mind. She ordered herself to be constructive. The engraved cufflinks. Engraving. What would happen if someone were to steal Henri's precious antique cufflinks? They would blame each other.

"Engraving!" she whispered. When she had lived in the convent, making rosaries, it was the practice to engrave on the back of gold crucifixes someone's name or a date, a legend of some kind. Initials usually. "Engraving!"

She remembered the story about two Nobel Prize medals: after the Nazis had invaded Denmark George de Hevesy was in possesion of medals won by two German physicists. It was a grievous offense to remove gold from the Fatherland and a group of Nazi searchers was on its way to de Hevesy's laboratory to retrieve the medals. He had no way to hide them but he was damned if he'd let the Nazis have them. So he made Aqua Regia, the only compound that could dissolve gold, and he dropped the medals into the liquid. The Nazis searched and searched but found nothing. The flask of gold-containing liquid stood innocuously on the shelf. After the war, the gold was recovered from the flask and the Nobel Committee had it cast into the two original medals. She had used Aqua Regia when engraving those gold crosses.

Was there hydrochloric acid on the laboratory shelf? And nitric acid, too? She brought her hands down to the back of her knees and sat down, bent forward, and slipped her hands under her feet. Now, with her hands in front, she unwrapped her ankles and using her teeth, she pulled at the edge of the tape that bound her wrists. In a minute, her hands were free.

On the shelf there was a nearly full bottle of hydrochloric acid. She continued searching and found a half bottle of nitric acid. She took an empty flask and filled it with three parts of hydrochloric acid and one part of nitric acid. She opened the drawers. She found several large assayer's magnets in one drawer. The screen door in the kitchen was a sturdy wooden door with a metal throw bolt. With a magnet, providing it was near a metal that would respond to it, she could pull back the bolt on the kitchen door.

The moon was still only a crescent moon, but along with the starlight, it would be bright enough for her to find her way without stumbling. She hoped that it would not become cloudy.

She waited until she believed that everyone in the house was asleep. Then she wrapped the tape she had removed from her wrists and ankles around her feet to act as shoes and crept up to the house. She held the magnet near the bulbous head of the sliding bolt. Slowly she drew the magnet across the door's frame until the bolt was clear of the jamb. She gently pulled open the door and let herself into the kitchen. There, on the counter, were the jewel boxes that they had opened and discussed earlier in the evening.

She picked up the red velvet cufflink box, opened it, and removed the golden objects and set the velvet box down in a different place so that it would be sure to be noticed. Knowing that the front door did not have a dead-bolt, but rather an ordinary key and spring lock, she re-locked the kitchen screen door and tiptoed into the living room where she quietly let herself out of the house. The lock made a noise as it snapped into place. She flattened herself against the front of the house in case someone had heard it and came to investigate the noise. After a minute, when no one came, she walked back to the lab and dropped the cufflinks into the aqua regia. She repositioned the bottles. Then she realized that they would surely come looking for the cufflinks and they would find the torn-off tape. She took the torn pieces and rolled them in the dust and dirt until they were convincingly nothing more than old trash that had lain behind a cabinet.

She picked up the spool of tape, bound her wrists, tore off a piece of tape with which she could bind her ankles, and after placing the spool exactly where Eric had left it, she returned to the cot, bound her ankles, and put her feet through the loop she made of her arms, and brought her bound hands up behind her.

She was too excited to sleep. The kitten curled up beside her ear and began to purr. "Thank you, Lord," she said. "I don't deserve your kindness."

THURSDAY, MARCH 1, 2012

Eric had come into the kitchen early. He was encouraged by Lilyanne's apology and wanted to make amends by preparing a nice breakfast and sitting down with her in the morning sun on the patio to share their meal together. Quietly, he lit charcoal briquets over his small barbecue and put a pot of water on to boil for breakfast tea.

Since he had no refrigerator it was necessary to buy food often and to consume it quickly. Usually, he traveled up and down the difficult road late every afternoon. He'd take his rubber sling speargun to get a fish for dinner and carry an encased pneumatic speargun to use in the event of a shark attack. To keep cream, butter and yogurt cold, he would use an insulated bag in which he kept one of two gel ice-packs. The hotel would keep one gel-pack in its freezer and daily he would exchange it for one that had reached its cooling limit in the bag. For fruits and vegetables he followed the practice of most cooks who live in rustic houses in the tropics: he would store them in a basket that hung from the ceiling on a string so that rats and mice could not get to them. The system was adequate for his needs.

On this morning, he had just enough eggs for one large omelet, yogurt and sliced fruit, and two rolls that he could butter and season and toast slightly over the flame. Charlotte had brought food with her, but the three of them had consumed it at dinner along with the mahi mahi. They would either have to open a can of something or go down to the hotel.

As the water for tea heated, he began to prepare the special platter of fresh fruit. He got a glass dish from the cupboard and the bowl for yogurt that fit into its central groove. He reached into his insulated bag, but it held only butter and a container of cream. Someone had taken the yogurt. He put the little bowl back into the cupboard and decided to serve just sliced fruit on the platter.

But when he reached into the basket to get the melon, oranges, and a bag of berries, he discovered that the oranges and the bag of berries were gone. It angered him that his guests had helped themselves to his food without so much as telling him. He took the boiling tea water off the stove and filled the tea pot, scrambled the eggs, put butter into the frying pan, and began to slice and arrange the melon. He poured the eggs into the pan and finished slicing the melon when suddenly, a piercing scream came from the kitchen. As he turned, another high-pitched shriek sounded and he bolted into the kitchen. "What is it?" he yelled.

"Aiiiiiah!" Henri screamed again. "Aiiiiah!"

Eric looked around frantically for blood or a body, for something that could account for the screams. He could find no cause. He grabbed Henri. "What's wrong?" he demanded to know. "What is it?"

Henri sat at the table pulling his hair and crying, "*Mommá! Mommá!*"

What he said next was so garbled Eric could not interpret in any of the languages he knew. Eric pleaded, "You're not making sense! What's wrong?"

Charlotte rushed in from the bedroom, disheveled and clothed only in a bed sheet and sandals. "What's wrong?" she shouted. Then, with a great wail, Henri held up the empty cufflink box. Charlotte gasped. "What happened to your cufflinks?"

Henri stopped sobbing to beat his fists on the table. "They're gone! They're gone!" He pointed at Eric and squealed, "He took them!"

"You're crazy!" Eric shouted. "What the hell would I want with your stupid cufflinks?"

Henri hissed malevolently. "You've always been jealous of me and my lineage!"

"Maybe Martin's looking at them," Charlotte said.

"Your *lineage*? Don't make me laugh!" Eric countered.

"Martin was with me all night." Henri shrieked. "He doesn't have them. They're gone. Eric or that Lilyanne freak stole them!"

"You leave her out of it," Eric demanded. "She's been in the lab all night. I had to unlock the kitchen door myself this morning."

Henri got up. "I'm going to the lab and make her give them back to me!"

Eric blocked his path. "Like hell you are." He shoved Henri back into a chair just as he smelled the omelet burning. "Son of a bitch!" he shouted, running back to the patio.

Charlotte began to pull out drawers and crawl on the floor looking under cabinets. "They've got to be here someplace!" she said, stumbling over her bed sheet. "Who was in the kitchen last night?"

Eric bounded into the kitchen holding the hot handle of the frying pan which he flung into the sink. "Take care of your own shit! Look what you've done! The eggs are ruined!"

Charlotte was indignant. "You want us to worry about your stupid eggs when our heirloom cufflinks are gone?"

Martin came into the room. "What is all this noise about!" he demanded to know. "I'm a sick man! I need my rest and don't need to wake up to all this screaming!"

"Someone took Henri's heirloom cufflinks!" Charlotte snapped. "This is serious! That jewelry has been in our family for generations! My God!" she cried. "We've got to find them!"

"Eric's 'wife' took them," Martin announced. "She must have come in here and taken them while we were sleeping."

"Shut your mouth, you two-faced prick!" Eric shouted. He turned to Henri. "Ask Martin where they are. He's the goddamned thief!"

"That's right," Martin said sarcastically. "Blame the black man!"

"Oh my God!" Charlotte hissed. "Are you introducing race into this catastrophe? Haven't you brought enough grief to our group?"

Martin smirked. "Lo! How the mighty have fallen. Look at you! Crawling on all fours! Do something worthwhile. Get me my morning coffee." He turned again to Eric. "Use your brain. Your so-called wife took them."

Eric was furious. "Lilyanne is in the lab. I bound her wrists and ankles. I took her shoes." He pointed at a corner of the kitchen floor.

"Look! I put them there last night! Nobody can walk across that gravel barefooted. And the kitchen door was locked! I had to unlock it myself this morning."

"Then she had a key to the front door," Charlotte said in a smarmy voice that irritated Eric further. He looked out on the patio to see that in the confusion he had not covered the melon slices and a dozen flies were crawling on the plate. "God damn you all!" he shouted, rushing out to see what he could salvage from the mess. The two rolls were in a bag. He brought the bag in and tossed it up into the basket. "And who the hell ate the oranges and the berries that were in here?" he asked.

No one answered. "Who stole the oranges and bag of berries?" he demanded.

Charlotte huffed. "I cannot believe that you'd be worried about fruit when heirloom jewelry is missing."

"Fuck your heirloom jewelry! Who ate my yogurt, oranges and berries?" Eric instinctively picked up the gutting knife that lay on the sink.

"Where's my coffee?" Martin demanded, looking at Charlotte.

"Get it yourself!" she shouted. "You're not some honored guest around here!"

"I guess I'm not any kind of guest in this dump," Martin whined. "A guest would be welcomed to a handful of berries! And I also need Vitamin C. But my medical needs are of no consequence to anyone around here."

"So you're the one who stole the fruit," Eric shouted. "You arrogant prick!"

Henri screamed, "Stop it! Stop it!" He positioned himself protectively in front of Martin. "My precious cufflinks are gone and all you care about is berries and eggs!"

"And yogurt and two oranges!" Eric corrected him. "You son of a bitch! I guess you ate one of them!"

"And what if I did?" Henri said defiantly.

Martin sat down and struck the table with the palm of his hand. "Why isn't coffee being served?" He looked at Charlotte. "You disrupted my sleep and now you deny me coffee! Tell our cheap host to make us some coffee."

"Don't look at me to beg Eric for your coffee!"

"Listen to the whore of Babylon talking," Martin sneered. "For all the service you've given him he ought to give me Irish coffee."

Charlotte was livid. "Go down to the hotel and order it, you piece of shit! I am not your slave! You duplicitous child-molester! I am so sick of looking at you, of listening to you, of having to talk to you in that mewling voice. They ought to re-open Devil's Island and put child-molesting scum like you in it!"

"Mammá! Aren't things bad enough? Do you have to make these outrageous remarks about Martin?"

"Outrageous? You simpleton! You've been replaced! He has a new boyfriend! Along with his line of bullshit he gave the kid AIDS."

Martin raised his arm as if preparing to strike her. "You lying whore!"

Eric pounded on the table. "Will all of you get the hell off my property! Get out! All of you! As of this moment you are trespassing!" Martin did not move; and Henri stood beside him, saying nothing as they listened to Charlotte.

"I'll show you! I'll show you!" she shouted as she ran back into the master bedroom and returned carrying the skirt into which she had crammed the letters and copies. "Well, Well, Well," she said, pulling the letters out, "we'll just see who is the lying whore! Here are his love letters... pathetic little love letters from children. He promises them the moon to get them to play with him. He is disgusting!"

Martin lunged for the letters. "Where did you get these? Copies? They're fakes... copies of fakes!"

Charlotte was defiant. "I'm sending the originals to the Namibian police! They'll put you in chains!"

"They were letters from Martin's friends!" Henri stamped his foot in defiance. "They're helping him with assays on minerals!"

As Charlotte, stunned into seeking divine assistance, raised her hands in prayer, the sheet slid to the floor. "My God! My God! Do not let my blessed husband see what an idiot sprang from his sacred loins." She turned to Henri. "Grow up! You bloody fool! You're a man! A thirty-five year old man! This monster has turned you into his pussy-boy! Here!" she produced an original letter. "This one's not a copy. It just came. He tested positive for AIDS. Do you really think the sick child wrote to him to tell him he had a bad assay test? What the hell does pyrite have to do with diamonds? You fool!"

"Where did you get that letter, you conniving bitch!" Martin lunged again for the letter which Charlotte held up in the air, providing a complete view of her naked breasts and pubic hair. "That letter was in my 'private drawer' on the Sesame! How did you get into my private papers?"

Charlotte danced and waved the letters.

"Get out!" Eric shouted again. "All of you! Get the hell off my property!"

Martin lunged at the table and succeeded in grabbing the letter. "How dare you go through my private papers! I ought to kill you, you white trash bitch!"

"Aaaaah!" Charlotte sucked in air, appalled by the accusation. She fiercely looked at Henri, pulling more originals out of her skirt. "Read the letters! He was going to the Namib to live with his boy... little Punye Abados." She placed a small stack of airmail letters on the table.

Henri ran out onto the patio with the letters. Charlotte and Eric stood in the doorway and prevented Martin from following him. Martin shouted through the screen door, "Those letters don't mean anything. They're kids. Stupid kids."

Charlotte stood in the doorway, knuckles on the sides of her waist, naked and acting as though it were normal to display her breasts and pubic hair in front of a screen door.

Eric collapsed in a chair and held his head. "Will you all get out... just get out. All of you. Out!"

Martin shouted to Henri, "Go to the lab. That's where you'll find your cufflinks. That bitch out there took them last night. She probably had a key."

Eric leapt out of the chair and ran out onto the patio. "No you don't!" he shouted.

Henri wiped his eyes and nose on his sleeve and staggered towards the lab. "Let's just settle it. We won't touch her or anything. We'll just ask her if she's seen my cufflinks... my beautiful cufflinks! They were given to me by my Papa!" Charlotte ran to support him.

"What are you afraid of?" Martin followed Eric outside, scoffing at him. "Are you afraid of what we'll find if we go and search her?"

Eric ran to get to the laboratory before the others could get there.

He stood at the lab door and allowed Henri and Charlotte to enter. "You," he said to Martin, "are not permitted near my wife!" He went to Lilyanne's bed and pulled the sheet up from her feet. "Her purse is in the house," he said, and so are her shoes! Look at her feet! They're bound! Do they look cut and bruised?" Then, as if he had just noticed that Charlotte was naked, he cried, "Go put some clothes on, for Christ's sake! Is that anyway to parade around in front of my wife!" He strode across the floor and took Charlotte's arm to lead her out of the room.

Henri noticed movement under the sheet. It was the kitten, but as if he expected to find Lilyanne trying to hide the cufflinks, he reached down and pulled the sheet off her. "Caught you!" he yelled.

"Eric!" Lilyanne cried in alarm.

Eric shouted, "Don't you touch her! You might be diseased too, you freak!" Eric picked up a shovel and advanced toward Henri. "Get out of this room and get off my property! I don't want you near my wife!" Henri squealed and ran to the doorway.

Martin pushed the door open. "You... you Viennese upstart!" he shouted at Eric as Henri ran into his arms. Martin pushed him aside and stepped into the laboratory. "And I've just about had enough of your insults," he shouted at Eric. "A man with breeding would have made coffee for his guests!" He raised his cane.

Charlotte tried to block Martin from entering the lab, but he slammed the cane down onto her instep. "You son of a bitch!" she screamed, hopping on one foot.

"Did it break your toe?" Martin taunted. "Good! *Wunderbar!*"

Eric raised the shovel and advanced towards the three of them. "I'll kill you all!" he bellowed. They ran to the house and Eric dropped the shovel. He sat on the edge of the cot and held Lilyanne. He unbound her wrists and ankles. "What am I going to do? My Lord, have I died and gone to hell? And yesterday we were so happy!" He got up. "Wait here," he said. He picked up the shovel and returned to the kitchen.

Martin had a few personal items in the room he had slept in. He gathered them and marched into the kitchen. "I'm taking Tommy and the Sesame, and you," he said to Charlotte, "can stay here with your irritating idiot of a son whose presence I can barely tolerate. Stay out of my way, all of you! Or the next time I lay eyes on you, I'll aim a shotgun at you."

Charlotte had not wanted to play her trump cards yet, but she had no choice. "You're not taking Tommy anywhere. You're not taking my ship anywhere. Yes, you ignorant peasant! I own Sesame. You own nothing. Nothing! And I deep-sixed those flash drives you were supposed to destroy! You conniving sneak! Oh, yes. I got your power of attorney and I cleaned you out. You've got nothing! No money! No skimmed pouches of jewels! Check the Maritime Registry. I own Sesame!"

Martin lunged for the speargun, picked it up, and aimed it at Charlotte. As Henri screeched, "Not my momma!" Martin pulled the trigger. Nothing happened.

"Idiot!" Eric shouted. "Do you think I'd leave a loaded speargun in my fucking kitchen!"

Martin swung the speargun at Henri who stepped back to avoid the blow and backed himself into a group of razor-sharp spear tips that hung on a loop against the wall. He screamed in pain as blood dripped from the cuts.

Charlotte picked up the empty bottle of champagne and swung it at Martin's head. She hit him over the left ear, opening the skin. Blood gushed out. "Oh, my God!" Eric shouted at the sight of Martin's blood. "Get him outside!"

Stunned, Martin collapsed onto the floor.

Charlotte leapt to the sink and scooped up a handful of the burned eggs from the frying pan. She leaped back onto Martin, pressed his nostrils together, and stuffed the eggs down into his throat. "Die! You child-molesting pig!" She pushed his chin up to keep him from spitting out the eggs.

Martin struggled, trying to pry Charlotte's hands off his face, until Henri intervened and grabbed both of Martin's hands and held them back against the floor. Eric passively watched as Martin died. By Eric's watch, it had taken only three minutes, total, for Martin to be absolutely dead.

Eric went into the bathroom to get bandages for Henri's wounds. Charlotte, still naked, helped to pull down Henri's pants to access the wounds. "My boy!" she cried. "My boy!"

"Do you really have all of Martin's assets?" Henri asked.

"For Christ's sake!" Eric again admonished Charlotte, "don't touch Henri while you've got Martin's blood all over you. Will you please go take a shower and put some clothes on!"

Eric washed his hands. "I'll bandage your wounds," he told Henri. "Just do yourself a favor and keep your mouth shut!"

Henri could not sit down and had to lean across the table. He was still lying there while Eric tried to make butterfly bandages to close the largest cut. Charlotte, clean and dressed, entered the kitchen. "Do you have a spare pair of jeans he can wear?" she asked Eric. "His clothes are in the Sesame."

"Look in one of the bedroom drawers. Give him an old pair." He looked at Martin. "And drag his body out of this room. Put him in the wheelbarrow outside. I have things that I need to do now."

Eric washed his hands again and took Lilyanne cold tea and two buttered rolls. "I'll be going down to the hotel to get you your food," he said. "We have a little broiled fish left over for Brynhilde. I don't know what their plans are. I'll get rid of them." He kissed her on the cheek and returned to the kitchen.

Charlotte restated her deal. "If you want the money and the boat, get him down the hill just as he is and call for emergency services. Same story. You were out in the yard and didn't hear anything and he choked to death on the kitchen floor... he had flung himself down struggling. I don't have any more of my Harriet rags and dental plate. You'll have to say he was staying with you because he was angry with me. He didn't want to leave the Caymans. You can say the yacht was a final payoff from me for money we owed you from the African mission supply account. If you take the boat and the money, we can use our van Aken papers and take the Piper to Cancun. If you don't want the boat and the money, we can take Tommy down to the airport and then as soon as Henri's wound is healed enough so that he and I can sail the ketch, we'll be off."

"No. No way," Eric said. "You killed him and you handle his death. Tommy knows you brought him here. The people who own the hotel know, too. They'll be asked."

Henri had a suggestion. "Why don't you two bury him at sea? Get him down to your boat... maybe you've hidden it where Tommy can't see it. Or if he sees you sailing out of the bay, Momma can tell him that Martin is up here with me. Helping to get rid of him ought to be worth a few hundred thousand dollars. When you get back, you can send Tommy home in a plane. In another day or so, my behind should be healed enough. I'm stronger than I look."

Eric cursed them all under his breath. "I want $300K from the sale of the house and all of the jewels and jewelry that were in Martin's box. You have plenty of jewelry. My wife has none - much of what he skimmed was stolen from her, anyway."

Charlotte got up and went into the bedroom and returned with the box. "It's all yours, except..." she opened the box and drew out the few remaining letters. "We must give Henri something to read... he needs an education about people you can't trust. Then we have a deal?" Charlotte said, placing the half-dozen baggies of diamonds and emeralds on the table.

Eric picked up the baggies. "I'm giving them to Lilyanne right now. Start wheeling Martin to the top of the road."

He put the bags of jewels into Lilyanne's tote bag, made a little dish of left-over fish, and walked to the lab and pushed open the door. "I have something for you," he said, handing her the tote bag. "Look inside and you'll find little bags of jewels... some are probably the very ones Martin pried out of the pieces you wore that night." He fed the kitten.

Lilyanne did not care about jewels. She sat up. 'I have to go to the bathroom." Eric picked her up and carried her to the outhouse.

"Please don't get mixed up with those people," she said, sitting on the hole. "Hand me the toilet paper. And I heard all the arguments. They're crazy."

Eric reached up and took a roll of toilet paper from the shelf. "I didn't have anything to do with Martin's death. She cleaned him out and he went crazy."

"Eric, she's lying if she says she doesn't have her Harriet Williams disguise. She intended to take Martin's body back to George Town. I heard her say so."

Eric thought for a moment. "That's right... that's what she said. So she's playing me again."

"Call the police and let them handle it."

"Sure. And let them take you away. You're being silly now. To save her ass she'd blame me for every crime the gang ever committed. No. I've got to get rid of his stinking carcass. I don't want the stench of him up here. He got blood on the kitchen floor. I have to disinfect the kitchen before you can go into it." He picked her up and carried her back to the lab.

Charlotte and Henri had dumped Martin's body into the wheelbarrow. His head had already attracted flies as he lay curled up inside it. As Eric approached the kitchen he could see and hear the flies buzzing around Martin and he could also see Charlotte and Henri as they huddled together, speaking in a confidential manner. "Come on, Charlotte," he said. "Let's get Martin down to my boat." He turned to Henri. "I'm leaving you here to guard my wife. If anything happens to her while I'm gone, I'll hunt you down and kill you... you and your mother."

"He'll guard her!" Charlotte gave her imperial assurance. "He's no fool. You know that you can trust Henri." Charlotte grabbed the backpack in which she had carried all her cash, papers, jewel boxes, and the contents of Martin's safe deposit box.

"Why do you need that?" he asked. "Can't Henri guard the bag? What do you have on your mind that you want to bring the money with you?"

"Nothing," she protested. "Here!" she tossed the heavy bag onto the kitchen table. "It was just force of habit. Ok. Let's get him down to the water."

"Go empty his pockets," Eric said. "I have to help Lily." He picked up her shoes and left the house. In the laboratory, he placed Lily's shoes beside her bed. "Stay in here. Henri will be here in the house. Don't antagonize him. They're all crazy."

Charlotte and Henri rifled the dead man's pockets and removed his passport and other articles.

Eric returned to the kitchen. "I've got the Remittman in a little cove under some camouflage netting. When we get half way down the path there's a little footpath that leads to the cove. Let's get started."

George's plane landed at Kirkconnell International airport on the tiny island. He tipped the pilot and hurried to an idle cab. "Do you know Claus van Aken's place?" he shouted as he approached the cabbie.

"Yeah, sure. Past Dennis Foster and Major McDonald roads. Get in."

George had not realized how small the island was. "What's the size of this island?" he asked.

"In miles? 12 by 1. You can run around it and still not do a marathon." In a few minutes, he deposited George at the small bayside hotel. "Here you are, safe and sound."

"Where's van Aken's place?" George asked as he paid him.

"That path over there," the driver pointed, "says Porter's Mining. Just climb to the top and you'll see Claus's place."

George hurried along the path. The sun became hotter as it approached noon. Half way up he had to stop and rest. His knee was beginning to throb. He didn't mind the pain but he knew that his leg could easily cramp and he'd be immobilized. He sat on a large rock at the side of the path and let his leg straighten out and relax. He waited five minutes and when the distress subsided, he continued on. Near the summit, he stopped again. He wanted to be fully mobile when he got to the top.

He saw Eric's house and garden. He heard noises coming from the rear and circled around to the patio area. Through a screened window he could see Henri in the kitchen, pulling open drawers, pulling dishes out of cabinets, mumbling something that George could not interpret.

Finally, Henri, talking to himself in a kind of frenzied dialogue, rushed out of the kitchen towards a grey wooden building. As soon as Henri entered the grey building, George entered the kitchen. He first saw the gutting knife Lilyanne had bought. He put it into his belt and looked around. On the side of the room, he saw the unloaded speargun lying on the floor. "Thank God," he whispered. "I've finally got a weapon." Spearguns were weapons that George had used a dozen years before when he and his brother used to sail to Bermuda to scuba dive and fish. But he could see no shafts to load into the gun. A cluster of arrow tips was in the sink, but without the shafts, they were useless. He also saw a protective case propped up on the floor against a cabinet. George recognized it immediately as the case of a pneumatic speargun carried only as a defense against sharks. He quietly opened the case and found the fully loaded weapon. He gently closed the case and picked it up, carrying it under his arm as he went through the house, softly calling, "Lilyanne.... Lilyanne..."

Screams and shouts started to come from the grey building. The screams were Lilyanne's. George knew her voice. He ran to the building.

Henri was standing over Lilyanne holding her hair in his left hand and a bottle of liquid in his right. "Where are my cufflinks!" he shouted. "Tell me or I'll pour this acid all over your pretty little face. You took them!"

"I don't know where they are!" She tried to pull his hand away from her hair. "You're hurting me! Let me go! I don't know where your cufflinks are!" she pleaded. "I don't have them."

George uncased the speargun and stood in the doorway, poised to use it. But first he had to get Henri away from Lilyanne.

"Your cufflinks are on the kitchen table," he said calmly. "I just put them there, myself."

Henri was confused. "I know who you are. You're the P.I. from Tarleton."

"That's right. Eric hired me to play the little cufflink joke on you."

"Eric? I should have known. Let's just bring her and make sure!" Still holding Lilyanne's hair, he tried to drag her from the bed. As she screamed and struggled he dropped the bottle of acid. Immediately smoke rose from the splashed area and the room filled with the choking fumes of acid. He continued to pull on Lily's hair, trying to drag her into the spilled acid. George pointed the speargun at him and fired, pinning Henri's chest to the wooden wall.

Lilyanne was crying. George picked her up. She tried to kiss his neck. George asked, "Who else is on the premises?"

"Brynhilde! Get my kitten Brynhilde!" The kitten ran into the jumble of implements in the rear of the room.

"Lily! We've got to get moving. I'm not armed! Who else is on the premises?"

"Nobody. Eric and Charlotte went to take Martin's body to the ocean to dispose of it." Her tote bag was on the counter. She reached over and grabbed its handles. "I don't know when they'll be back."

"Do you have your passport?" George asked.

"No, it's in the house." She led him into the kitchen and opened a drawer in a cabinet. She removed her passport and pushed it down into her tote bag.

George carried her to the slippery path and set her down. "Let's go," he said. "I've only got a knife on me."

As quietly as possible they slip-slided down the path. At the halfway point, George heard a faint rumbling noise coming from a footpath that branched off from the main path. He pulled Lilyanne down behind some large rocks and through some foliage saw Eric coming towards them, pushing an empty wheelbarrow.

George pulled the knife out of his belt. "Now's my chance to get this son of a bitch!" He stood up.

Lilyanne grabbed his arm. "No! Let him go!"

George looked down at her quizzically. "I can take him!"

"No! Let's just go on." She pulled on his sleeve and he stooped down again, hiding until Eric had turned onto the main path and headed up towards another switchback.

The switchbacks were such that the moment Eric turned again in their direction, he would be able to see them. George stood up and saw that Eric's back was to him as he headed towards the switchback's curve. He grabbed Lilyanne. "We can get another fifty feet down before he reaches the turn."

They continued and then dropped down behind some foliage to hide until Eric had reached the end of that section of road and had to turn, continuing the climb to the top.

They ran into the hotel. George took out his cellphone and called Everett Smith. "I've got her!" he said. "We're on Cayman Brac. I'll have to see about getting a flight to George Town. From there I'll get us two tickets and with any luck we'll be home tonight or tomorrow or maybe even after we spend a few days together in Miami. Here! I'll let Lilyanne talk to you." He handed her the phone. She cried and babbled incoherently as George went to the desk clerk.

"Do you happen to know that Porter's road that goes up to the top?"

"Sure."

"There's a little footpath that branches off it. Where does that go?"

"To a cliff that's over vertical. You have to rapel down to the water. Tide's in so probably there are many sharks in the water there. They like to congregate and feed on the big lizards that hang out there."

Lilyanne called him. "Daddy wants to talk to you."

George answered and Everett Smith said, "I'm sending a private jet from Cancun in the Yucatan. Do not leave her side for a single minute. I'll call you when I get the plane's e.t.a."

"All right," George replied. "But we'll be on our way to George Town."

"Yes. That's where I'm having the jet meet you. It'll refuel in George Town and then land in Philadelphia by tonight. Good job, George!"

"Thanks," he said, feeling rebuffed about his expressed hope that they might spend a few days in Miami. "Just let me know when it's gonna land in George Town."

The cabbie who had brought George from the airport was still at the hotel, finishing his lunch. "Do you folks want a ride back?" he asked.

"You bet we do," George said, swooping Lilyanne up in his arms and carrying her out to the cab. "Don't say a word in the cab," he cautioned. "We don't want to be involved in testimony about what went on back there. I want to get you out of the country as soon as possible."

All the way to the airport, George had his arm around her, delirious at being able to kiss the top of her head and, when she put her head on his shoulder, to rub his cheek against her hair.

A flight to George Town was boarding as they arrived at the airport. George asked them to hold the door open for just long enough for them to use his credit card. In another minute he handed two boarding passes to the flight attendant and he and Lilyanne settled into two seats, one three seats behind the other.

Finally, at 4 p.m. George and Lily opened the door of Room 413 of the Lamark Hotel. He wanted to kiss her. He expected to kiss her. He put his arms around her and pulled her to him; but she resisted. "What is it?" he said. "What's wrong?"

"I'm a mess," she said. "I'm dirty and I'm starving. I haven't really eaten anything substantial since last night."

"You look fine to me," he said, confused by the apparent rejection. "But we can order food and have it sent up." He picked up the hotel phone and dialed the room-service number. "What do you want to eat?"

She picked up the menu as he handed her the phone. "It'll have to be something fast," she said, "since we don't know when the jet will get here." While she spoke to room-service, he went into the bathroom and closed the door. He leaned against the sink and stared in the mirror. "What's goin' on?" he asked his reflection. He thought about the handsome blonde man who had held her captive. "I wanted to kill the guy, but she stopped me," he explained to his reflection. "She didn't say anything when I killed Henri; but this guy was different. She didn't want him hurt. Did she fall for him, or what? And what was that kitten all about? He left her alone and unbound, playing with a kitten! What's goin' on?"

The image stared back at George and said nothing. But the bulbs around the medicine cabinet had plenty to say. In their glare he could see the crow's feet at the corner of his eyes. That masculine ruggedness - the handsome man gracefully aging - was nowhere to be found. He stared at the worry lines between his eyebrows. They were as ugly on his face as the hideous furrows left in the earth by strip mining. "Well, you idiot," he told his reflection, "you accomplished what you were hired to do. A servant P.I. Pick up your pay and don't get any ideas about becoming part of the family."

A sudden inclination to cry swelled in his throat. He gulped it down and turned on the shower. He stripped off his clothing and stood under the water. He did not even notice that he had turned on only the cold water. He used the little shampoo and creme rinse bottles, "For sea and sun damaged hair." He finished his shower, toweled off, shaved, blow dried his hair, and put all his toiletries into their traveling bag. He "respectfully" - since, after all, he was in his employer's presence - wrapped a bath towel around himself and went into the bedroom to get fresh clothing.

"I ordered the same thing for you," she said. "Cheeseburgers and fries. I hope that's ok."

"Sure. Thanks."

"I'm going over to my room to see if my things are still there."

"Wait a minute. Tell me what's wrong."

"I don't want to talk about it. It was a very difficult time for me."

"For me, too!" He suddenly felt angry. "I didn't realize I was trying to rescue a stranger. Maybe I wouldn't have tried so hard." He picked up his clothes and went into the bathroom to put them on.

"George," she protested, but he shut the door.

His phone rang. Lily called, "Should I answer it?"

"Yes."

He heard her say, "Yes, Daddy. Oh, Thank you Daddy. Forty-five minutes? I'll just have time to eat and be at the airport." She called to George. "The private jet will be here in forty-five minutes. I can't wait to get home. I hope room-service gets here soon." She picked up her tote bag. "I have to see what's still in my room," she said, opening the door. He listened, and as the door closed behind her, a feeling of loss overwhelmed him.

So much for a few days spent loving and relaxing with him in Miami! He came out of the bathroom and folded his soiled clothes and put them in the plastic bag that had been in his closet. Then he put the bag in his carry-on suitcase along with his toiletry bag.

Where did he get the idea that at this precise moment they would be naked in bed making love and laughing and saying wonderful things and just being.... what? happy in love? happy to have found each other? Instead of laughing he felt as though he had inhaled a fifty pound stone. Its weight pulled down on his lungs, stifling him.

He picked up the phone and called the desk. "Would you prepare my bill. I just ordered room service. Add it to my tab but have it delivered to Room 412. Yes. I'll be right down."

He left his luggage in the open doorway. He could not leave without saying goodbye to her.

He crossed the hall to her room and found her sitting on her bed crying. He stood in front of her and asked again, "Please tell me what's wrong."

"George... I could be pregnant."

Relief drained from his head to his toes. "Is that what's bothering you?" He knelt on the floor in front of her. "What's the problem? You'll have a beautiful baby. You'll make a wonderful mother."

"It would be Eric's baby."

"Hey... a baby is a baby. They all look alike and they're all cute."

"A baby needs a father."

"I wouldn't suggest that you marry Eric, but there are probably ten million guys in a fifty mile radius of Tarleton who would jump at the chance to marry you and be that baby's father."

"Is there a P.I. among them?"`

"If you mean, a P.I. named Wagner, then yes... yes there is. Is this a proposal? Shouldn't you be the one who's down on one knee asking for my hand?" He was giddy, euphoric. He wanted to reach out and take her arms and stand up and pull her up to him. But she had begun to cry again and to reach to the bedside table for a tissue.

"If I'm pregnant then you'll marry me to make the baby legitimate? Oh, George! I am so grateful. You know my mother. A child born out of wedlock would be cause for her suicide." She blew her nose and looked up at him adoringly.

There was something troubling about her answer. The room service waiter knocked on the door. As George went to answer it, he turned and asked, "And if you're not pregnant?"

"Then there's no rush. I can take my time to get my nerves back in shape and gain some of the weight I've lost."

"I understand," he murmured. He wanted to shout that he understood all too well and then to castigate himself for being such a fool.

The waiter wheeled the cart into the room and placed it before Lilyanne. He lifted the silver domes from the platters. "Here you are, Miss," he said. "Enjoy."

Lilyanne looked up and saw that George wasn't in the room. Assuming that he had gone back to his room for something, she picked up her cheeseburger and took a bite. She chewed and swallowed and called, loud enough for him to hear across the hall, "I don't want to look like a scarecrow in a long white dress!"

But George had already entered the elevator. By the time she swallowed her second bite, he was going to the desk to pay his bill.